being

BARRY JONSBERG

here

ALLEN&UNWIN

The author and publisher would like to thank
Faber & Faber Ltd for permission to reproduce extracts
from the poem 'The Old Fools' published in
Collected Poems by Philip Larkin.

First published in 2011
Copyright © Barry Jonsberg 2011

Allen & Unwin
83 Alexander Street | Crows Nest NSW 2065 | Australia
Phone (61 2) 8425 0100 | *Fax* (61 2) 9906 2218
Email info@allenandunwin.com | *Web* www.allenandunwin.com

A Cataloguing-in-Publication entry is available from
the National Library of Australia www.trove.nla.gov.au

ISBN 978 1 74237 385 0

Notes for teachers available from www.allenandunwin.com

Design by Bruno Herfst | Set in 11.5 PT Caslon Classico
Printed in Australia by McPherson's Printing Group

10 9 8 7 6 5 4 3 2 1

THE END

At death you break up: the bits that were you
Start speeding away from each other for ever
With no one to see

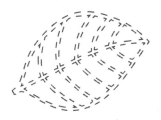

I face a window.

Beyond, there is grass and a sky dusted with clouds. It is a picture I almost remember. I see my face suspended in the pane, a ghost in the landscape. Sometimes, when nurses weave across the grass, pushing wheelchairs, they trace lines across my face. One nurse skims my upper lip.

Nurses don't wear white anymore. I'm told it is too cold. They are wrapped in blue, the colour of pinched veins.

It is difficult to keep my eyes open.

Some days are better than others.

Darkness congeals, thickens slowly into night.

I know who I am.

I know where I am.

It is not always like this.

No one visits. I have no family. At least when memories have fled entirely I will be spared the pain of not recognising a daughter, a son. That must be the worst.

On my good days, I know what the future holds.

Sometimes I gaze at my friend across the table and cannot pin her down, though I have known her for years. My mind chases a name, but it slips away, squirms and twists, a greased thing that cannot be held. What will happen when everything is like that? When the mind chases ghosts through half-remembered doors into half-remembered rooms and I turn and turn and realise the place I live is deserted? Of the living. And the dead.

When no one, truly, is at home?

They say you can achieve anything, provided you have the will to chase your dreams, face your fears and never give up.

They lie.

Lucy. My friend. Her name is Lucy.

'Hi! How you doin' Mrs Cartwright?'

It's one of my good days, but I don't know who she is. I am in the residents' lounge and she stands before me, moving her weight from one leg to the other as though the floor is scorching her feet. She is impossibly young. Dressed in jeans that defy gravity, exposing flesh to the point where imagination borders on redundant. A short red top with laces instead of straps. There is a blue streak in her hair, above her right ear. Something metallic glints in her left eyebrow. Just looking at her makes me feel twenty years older. This is something I can ill afford.

'Still breathing,' is the best reply I can muster. She smiles, exposing a curious contraption that hugs her teeth. It contains a good percentage of the primary colours. Is there a sound orthodontic reason for that?

'Excellent,' she says.

I wonder, briefly, how one can excel at breathing. Do I know this child? I suppose it doesn't matter.

'You remember me, right?' she asks, as if reading my mind. She frowns slightly and her eyebrow winks with light.

'No. Should I?'

'I came to see you last week. My name's Carly.'

She waits for a light bulb to appear over my head. It doesn't.

'A week is a long time in geriatrics,' I point out. 'Some days I can't remember who *I* am.'

'Oh, sure,' she says. 'Well. Right. Yeah.' I wonder if she is attempting a world record for consecutive mono-syllables, but then she disillusions me. 'It's just that last week you said I could interview you. For my Social Education project. Remember? I'm a Year 11 student at the Senior College and I have to write a report on local history. Research stuff.'

'I'm local history?'

'Sure. Well, I don't mean you're a fossil or anything.' I catch another glimpse of multi-coloured braces. 'But you're like ...' She screws up her forehead.

'Old?' I suggest.

'Yeah. Really old. And I reckon you'll have lots of memories of how things were in the past. My teacher, she thought it was a great idea. Said it would be a wel-come change from all that internet browsing. See, you're a primary resource, Mrs Cartwright.'

Her tone suggests I should be thrilled. At least she calls me Mrs Cartwright, though I've never been mar-ried. Most people just call me Leah and never consider the implications. Is it really acceptable for total strangers to use my first name? Does my being old give them licence? I understand it's meant to be friendly. It is not. It's familiarity that is close kin to contempt. At some point I became someone not to be taken seriously. Age strips you of everything. It tears you down, layer by layer. It's like erosion. Relentless. All it takes is the ticking of a clock.

The use of a title and my last name hints at respect. The child has bought herself some time.

'And you're, like, one of the oldest people in the state.' She's warming to her theme. 'I mean, how awesome is that?'

One of the disadvantages of living almost entirely in your head is the inability to let something go. Thoughts weave, spun from the most unpromising threads. A chance remark. And that image breeds associated images. Unlikely words spark pathways. 'Awesome.' It is not a word I would use to describe this sweet accident of living. It's an ancient pattern over which I have no control. Each breath comes of its own volition. And each breath is a step towards the darkest destination of all. That's true of every living thing. I cannot believe accumulating more years than most is an occasion for awe. The machine is winding down. I feel pain. Indignation. Sometimes resignation.

It's far removed from awesome.

'Awful' is a more appropriate word. But I nod.

'So what I thought we could do is just chat, you know. About the way things were. And if you don't mind, I could record what you say.' She takes a small machine from her bag and places it on the table in front of us. It is a challenge thrown down. 'Then, later, I can write up a report for my project. So all you have to do is talk. I mean, last week you said it would be okay. You haven't changed your mind or anything?'

Sometimes I can't find my mind, let alone change it. I keep the thought to myself.

'My life has been unremarkable,' I reply. 'In fact I have never set foot outside the state. I can't believe I would have anything of interest to say.'

'Yeah, but that doesn't matter. Seriously. My teacher said you'd be a great resource for me to find out how everyday lives were lived, like ages ago. So it doesn't have to be dramatic or anything. I just want the ordinary stuff, you know?'

'You want my memories?'

She nods.

'Before they wither and die?' I add.

Most adults think it is tactless to invite death into the room. They become embarrassed and can't meet your eyes. They don't realise that, for the old, death is a familiar companion, a presence that leans over your shoulder, its breath constantly on your neck. For this girl mortality is abstract, an entry in the dictionary. She grins.

'Yeah. Exactly.'

I smile. Her openness is attractive. And there are stories buried within me. One in particular. I don't know if this child will be interested in it. I don't even know if I can tell it. It is not about the ordinary. It's about the extraordinary. It's about the sweetness of life, the destruction we work, in the name of love, on those closest to us. It's about a boy, a girl, the power of imagination. And the muscles that stories flex. It's about a miracle.

Most of all, it's about the joy and pain of love.

'You want to start now?' I ask.

She nods. 'Hey, why not?'

'Sit,' I say. 'Switch on your machine.' She does both. A small red light glows.

They say time travel is an impossibility. They lie. I do it all the time. I think back to the girl I was. I do not become her. I cannot fill her skin or see through her eyes. The girl from the past is outside of me. And I am beside her. I observe and the story unfolds.

'They say good things come to those who wait,' I start. 'But they lie…'

CHAPTER 1

SHE WAS FIVE YEARS old when her father walked into the barn, put a shotgun into his mouth and pulled the trigger.

The girl stood framed in early morning light. Something was different about the inside of the barn, but she wasn't sure what. Maybe it was the texture of the silence. She took two steps forward. Her eyes squinted against the dark. The shadows were familiar. Rusted machinery parts, fence posts, bundles of wire and odd shapes covered with tarpaulin. Motes of dust danced in the sun's rays.

She took another step.

Her father was slumped against the back wall. A pattern of blood and brains was a bouquet against seasoned wood.

She took another step.

The farm was her world. The girl knew death. But this was different. She crouched by her father's splayed legs and tugged at his trousers. When nothing happened she stood and put one grimy thumb in her mouth. She remained for a couple of minutes, watching the flower spray that bloomed from the ruins of her father's head. She heard the buzz of blowflies.

Finally, she backed out of the barn and went in search of her mother. She didn't run. She didn't take the thumb from her mouth. The sun sweated. Dust puffed beneath her bare feet.

The girl was only five, but she understood that the world had shifted. Nothing would ever be the same again.

The men left. They took with them the strange bundle that used to be her father.

Her mother didn't cry. But she held her daughter for what seemed forever. The arms enfolding her were not gentle. The girl had difficulty breathing, so fierce was the grip. After a while, she squirmed from her mother's embrace and sat outside in the early afternoon sun. She hummed a small song.

The day grew old and noises from the house slipped under the door. She sat outside until the darkness came. For a time she was joined by Pagan, her border collie. He sat at her side and panted, lips drawn back as if laughing. The dog licked her legs with a tongue like a rasp. She giggled. When the day finally died, the girl went back into the house. She was hungry. She wanted her father to come home. She wanted the door to open, for him to kick off his work boots, pick her up and tickle her under her arms until laughter turned to sweet pain.

She didn't know it, but this was the beginning of a lifelong habit. The wish to wind back time and fix it. The sense of loss when time stubbornly spooled forward.

The house remained shadowy and empty. From her mother's room, a thin wail rose, like a pale flower growing in the dark.

'Books are alive,' said her mother. 'But only when you open them. They need you to bring them to life. Like Sleeping Beauty.'

The girl knew *Sleeping Beauty*. It was one of her favourites.

'She only had life when the Prince kissed her. You kiss a book by reading it. And the story stirs, shakes itself, becomes full of people and places and animals. A world grows around you. And that world is yours to explore each time you turn the page.'

The girl understood little of this. She was five years old. But she liked the idea of giving life to stories.

'I will write a story one day,' said her mother. 'And it will be perfect. The world I make will be so wonderful that we will never want to be anywhere else. I will write it for you.'

The girl wanted to ask her mother to make her father into a story. Then she could open his pages and bring him to life. But she was scared to ask. So she turned the pages of her book of fairytales, let her eyes kiss them and felt worlds shiver and stir.

The day of the funeral was stunned by heat. The girl stood on the verandah and watched the rows of apple trees. They were lined up as if for inspection. Their leaves didn't shiver or stir.

She wore her best dress, but it felt sticky, heavy against skin. She wasn't allowed to sit for fear of staining her dress. Pagan wasn't allowed to lick her legs. He didn't understand why and she couldn't tell him. She didn't know either.

There was a car and many people. She recognised some. Farmers from adjoining properties. Familiar faces from church. They were all dressed in fine clothes. Most looked the way she felt. She saw some tug at collars or mop faces. The girl had never seen so many people together at one time. It was like a scene from a book, a procession, a gathering. It should have been joyous, so many people. But instead it was dark. Men murmured, women wrapped arms around her mother's shoulders. Most people rested a hand on the girl's black curls, gave her a tired smile, tried to say something, but thought better of it. She didn't like the attention. Before long she wanted them to go away. They didn't.

It was her first car ride. The interior smelled of leather and polish. Each pothole in the dirt road sent jolts along her spine. When she looked back, the farm, framed in the rear window, was shrouded in dust.

The church was cool and familiar. So too the rows of hard seats. She sat at the front, next to her mother. People talked, but the stories they told didn't make sense. A beam of light, angled in from a high window, picked her out in rainbow colours, made her drowsy. She wanted to sleep, but knew that wouldn't be right. The girl sat straighter in her seat. Her bottom was aching and the light made her eyes narrow. She glanced over to the row of seats on the other side of the aisle.

He sat on the end furthest away from her. As she craned her neck to get a better look, he did the same. Their eyes met over ranks of pressed trouser legs and starched dresses.

His hair stuck out at strange angles. He wore long pants with holes in them and a stained work-shirt. She had never seen him before. He smiled at her. She smiled back.

When the people stopped talking, the girl took her mother's hand and stepped into sunshine. They drove home in silence, but her mother never once let go of her hand. It felt cold and clammy. Her mother's face glistened and she blinked many times. The girl wanted to let go, but knew she shouldn't. She wanted to be home, to find the cool darkness of her room and open a book. A special book. She had read it many times before, but never tired of it. It had a crisp world and almost everyone in it was happy.

So it was unpleasant to find that nearly everyone who had been in church had followed them back. Some came in rattly cars. Others in carts drawn by dust-coated horses. Her mother took the people into the house and brought out trays and trays of food. Everyone ate and talked in low voices. The girl had never heard so much talking in one day. She was tired of it.

She tugged at her mother's hem and asked — in a very small voice — if she could get changed out of her new clothes. Her mother, who was talking to a man in a dark suit, said she could.

'How can I explain this to her?' she said to the man. 'When I can't begin to explain it to myself.'

But the man only shook his head and glanced at his polished shoes.

'We must trust in the Lord,' her mother continued.

He nodded.

When the girl had changed, she didn't feel like reading. For some reason, the low rumble of conversation that carried into her room felt like a stain. She wasn't sure she could kiss worlds into existence against that background hum. So she stepped onto the verandah. Pagan uncurled himself from beneath a chair and sat beside her. He flicked his eyes up to hers and his tail thumped softly against the dusty boards. But he didn't try to lick her legs. The apple trees stretched into the distance, blushed now by a dipping sun. The day cooled. A light breeze brushed her cheek. She stepped off the verandah. Grass whispered against her shins.

The trees formed avenues. The girl allowed her eyes to drift over the rows until they settled on one, to her right. It wasn't a choice, as such. She never chose which avenue to explore. Her eyes fixed on one and that was the one she followed. And if she had been asked why she did this she wouldn't have been able to tell. There was no difference between the rows. They looked the same. They led to the same destination.

Pagan trailed her through the avenue.

The boy sat in the branches of the fifth tree on the left. She could see his scuffed boots dangling. But she kept her head down right up to the point when she came level. Then she stopped and turned her eyes up. He sat like an exotic fruit. His face was heavily freckled, his eyes large, brown and almond-shaped. His hair still stuck out at wild angles.

'Hello,' she said.

The boy didn't speak, but he smiled. And when he smiled a light turned on in his face.

'What's your name?' she asked. The boy shrugged. She sat cross-legged at the base of the tree and pulled out a blade of grass. She ripped it carefully up its spine, frowning as she did so. Pagan lay in a pool of dappled sun.

'I will call you Adam,' said the girl. 'Do you like that name?'

The boy shrugged again and pushed off from the branch. His boots landed a metre from her face. She didn't look up. She continued shredding the blade.

'Do you like stories?' she asked.

'Don't know,' said Adam. 'Never heard one.' He sat opposite her, crossed his legs and pulled a blade of grass. For a minute they were both absorbed, working finger-nails into green flesh.

'My favourite,' said the girl, without looking up, 'is about a cold land surrounded by mountains. There is a castle. A beautiful castle. It is the first thing travellers see when they come to the peak of the mountains. It is nestled in a green valley, where the cold can't touch. It is golden with sun. Everyone is happy there.'

She discarded the split blade of grass and plucked another. The boy did the same. Another minute passed.

'I've seen that place,' he said.
'Where?'

Adam used the blade of grass to point. His arm stretched further down their avenue of trees.

'There,' he said.

'Show me?'

Adam walked on one side of the avenue, the girl on the other. Pagan padded between them. The sun slid behind the earth and shadows grew from trees and changed the landscape. Darkness sprouted from the ground and the trees thickened and crowded. It was as if the path they trod narrowed so they were forced to come together. Branches drooped, the leaves and their shadows merged with one another. Dark walls rose.

Adam stopped. The girl glanced over her shoulder. She could no longer see the pathway through the trees. There was no sound, except their own breathing and Pagan's slow panting. Their breath misted against the darkness. The air was tingly with cold.

'Here,' said Adam, reaching forward and parting the darkness. He stepped through. She followed. Leaves caressed her as they parted. She burst into light.

They stood on the summit of a mountain. A dizzying drop yawned beneath. On all sides, ice and snow glittered. The girl glanced at her feet, a step from the brink. She shuffled backwards. The sky was powdered blue, dusted with wisps of cloud. The sun was swollen gold. The mountains ranged on all sides, but her eyes were drawn from them. Down, down, down into a patch of green in the valley below. A winding road, delicate as a pencil line on green paper, led to a castle, its walls buttery in light. A thin ribbon of moat sparkled. The turrets, four, five, six, pointed towards the heavens. Each was capped with red. From this height she could see no movement, but the girl narrowed her eyes and thought she saw the thin lines of windows in the walls. She knew that people moved there and she knew they were happy.

'Is there a way down?' she asked.

Adam brushed her arm. He pointed to their right where a pathway sliced through ice and snow and rock. It curved down, became lost in the bends, re-emerged lower in the valley. After a while, her eyes could no longer follow its descent.

'It's as beautiful as I imagined,' she said.

A voice came to her, faint as a memory. It called her name.

'I have to go back,' she said.

'I know,' said Adam.

She turned and the leaves were behind her, a wall of darkness. As she reached out, she thought for a moment she would encounter something that would not yield. But the leaves parted and blackness spilled out. The girl stepped through. She could feel Pagan's presence but she could barely see him. He was a shadow within shadows. She walked. And with each step the air became warmer. Breath stopped misting in front of her face. Within a minute she saw the outlines of trees, an avenue opening. The voice was louder now. Her mother's voice, calling.

Halfway along, she turned. She could no longer see Adam but she felt him there in the shadows.

'Don't leave,' she whispered. 'Don't leave.'

There was no reply, but she knew he had heard. She turned again. Through the thinning trees, the yellow lights of home glowed. She ran towards them, Pagan at her side. The darkness fell away.

When everyone had gone, the girl and her mother ate a simple meal. Afterwards, the girl was bathed and tucked into her mother's bed.

'I need you with me tonight, my angel,' said her mother. 'Just until we … get used to things.' Then she read her a story. But for once the girl didn't pay attention. She examined the walls of her mother's bedroom. Nothing had changed. The large wooden cross still floated over the bed-head. The pictures of the man with the bleeding heart and the crown of thorns. But change was there, all the same.

She thought about her father, but he was fading. It had only been five nights since he had slept in this very spot, but she could feel his presence drifting away. He seemed no more than a shadow now. Less solid than a story. Because a story could become dimmed, but it never died. It slept. Before too long her father would have no substance. He didn't sleep. Already, she could barely remember his face.

After the story, they knelt next to the bed and prayed. The ritual felt good. The coldness of floorboards against her knees. The recitation of words she didn't understand.

Later, the girl woke. The house ticked. Metal shrank in the cool of night. She felt the warmth of her mother's body next to her. She knew that if she turned, her mother's eyes would be open, that she would be trying to fix a face into the darkness. But she didn't turn. She kept her gaze on the far side of the bedroom. The moon was thin through curtains. All she could see were blocks of darkness stacked in random patterns. But as her eyes adjusted, the shapes resolved into a chest of drawers, the outline of a chair.

Adam sat in the chair. His legs swung, to and fro.

The girl smiled and closed her eyes.

'I am tired,' I say. 'I want to stop now.'

In truth, I have almost forgotten the child. Chasing ghosts along labyrinths of memory does that. It becomes difficult to distinguish what is real and what isn't. So when I focus on the now, when I tear myself from the then, it is a dislocation. The residents' lounge is leached of life. I feel ripped from a world of colour into something pale. As insubstantial as a thought.

The girl — I have forgotten her name — presses a button on the machine and the red light fades and dies. For a moment I wonder if I have spoken any words at all or if they've echoed only in my head.

'Hey, thanks, Mrs Cartwright,' she says, with unnatural cheerfulness. 'That's ... great. It's just ...'

'Yes?'

She bundles the machine back into her school bag, brushes a hand through her hair.

'Well ... it's not quite ... not quite what I need. For my project, you know? I mean, it's interesting and everything, what you said. But Miss Jones — my teacher — she's given us all these criteria. I'm meant to research social history. And what you're giving me is ... well, a story. Which is great for English. But not for Soc Ed. You see what I mean?'

I have disappointed her. I can't find it in myself to feel sorry. But I nod.

'So next time I'll ask you questions, like a question-naire,' she continues. 'Make sure I hit those criteria.'

'No,' I say. 'You won't.' I shift in my seat. Why does everything hurt? 'The only good thing about being old is that I can make my own rules. And stories are what I am interested in. What I've always been interested in. I do not have to do what anyone tells me. I please myself.'

She frowns and for a moment I think she is going to argue. But then a smile wipes her face clean. I am given another flash of her braces. It is as though she is chewing a rainbow.

'Make your own rules?' she says. 'I wish *I* could. I guess being old has earned you the right.' She delivers the cliché as if it's a profound truth.

'Being old,' I reply, 'earns you nothing.'

Her smile falters. She gets to her feet and shrugs her bag over one shoulder.

'If my story's not what you need, Carla,' I say, 'then I suppose I won't be seeing you again.'

'Carly,' she says. 'I'm Carly. And, hey, Mrs C, I'd like

to come back, if that's okay with you. I'll talk to my Soc Ed teacher. We'll figure something out.'

Mrs C?

'As you wish,' I say.

'What? Oh, right. It's just, if you want to tell a story, then hey. That's okay. Your rules.'

My nurse is here, tidying the residents' lounge. She has red hair and a husband whose eyes wander. I see him when he picks her up at the end of her shifts. He watches the other nurses. Sometimes he licks his lips. He is wrong and she knows it. But it never stops her smiling.

'Call first,' she says to the girl. 'Leah … Mrs Cartwright, well, you have your good days and your not-so-good days, don't you, sweetheart? It's best to check.'

She's right. Some days I'm buried so deep I cannot find the surface.

The girl moves around the table and puts her hand on mine. It is soft and lambent with youth.

'In your story, the boy, Adam?' she says. 'He's an imaginary friend, isn't he? Did I get that right? That's cool. One of my mates had an imaginary friend when she was little.'

'Oh, no,' I say. 'You don't understand. Adam wasn't imaginary. He was real.'

* * *

I lie in sheets that smell of old people. The faint tinge of urine, sweat and hopelessness. I listen to the intake of breath. One after the other.

Sometimes I wish I could just stop.

CHAPTER 2

'I HAVE DECIDED,' SAID LEAH's mother. 'I will not wait. I refuse to wait. Today, I will start my story. Do you remember, my angel? I said I would write a story that would be perfect, about a place where we would want to live forever.'

She washed the breakfast dishes. Energy poured from her. The air shimmered with it.

'So, I am going to write for three hours every day. Every day. And in the afternoon we will do our chores around the farm and play games. What do you say?'

The girl nodded.

'But Mummy will need quiet. Mummy will need peace and quiet to build her story. So while I am writing I need you to play by yourself. Do you understand?'

Leah nodded.

A little later, Leah gathered a pile of books and stepped out onto the verandah. Her mother sat at the kitchen table, crouched over a sheet of paper, a pencil in her hand. Her brows knitted as she stared at the expanse of white. She settled herself in the chair.

The girl closed the front door quietly. She sat on the steps and spread her books out. Her brows wrinkled too. Finally, she selected one. She opened it and the familiar picture was before her. Already, she could feel the people and the animals and the world stirring. They were asleep on the page, but her eyes were tickling them to life.

She read to Pagan. He lay in the dust at the foot of the stairs, one ear cocked as if to hear more clearly. The inside of his ear was white and stiff with wiry hairs. It was the story of the girl in the forest and the red house and the small animals that lived there and the threat brooding in the forest that would come when the sun dipped beneath the horizon. And though the girl knew how the story would end, she was never fully sure until she got there. Because she felt change was possible in any story, but the act of reading kept things the same. Her voice ensured everything turned out the way it should.

When she finished, Pagan twitched his ear.

'I have seen that place,' said Adam. He sat on the railings of the verandah. His legs swung, to and fro.

'Show me?' said Leah.

The days of summer flickered past. After a while it was difficult to see the joins. Routine smoothed them out.

Every morning after breakfast, Leah took her books outside. Or, if it rained, she took them to her bedroom. She read for three hours. Sometimes, when she tired of reading, she walked among the apple trees. But never far from home. Her mother had made her promise never to go far. She met Adam there. He would be sitting in a tree, or sitting on the grass, splitting blades. She read him stories. And Pagan, whose love was unconditional, was always by her side.

At midday she returned to the house. Her mother folded up her writing materials and placed them carefully in a box which she locked. Then she prepared food. They ate on the verandah and talked.

'Can you read me your story, Mummy?' the girl often asked, but the response was always the same.

'Not yet, angel. Not yet. It takes a long time to write a story and even longer to make it perfect.'

After a month, the girl stopped asking.

In the afternoons, they usually did chores together. Housework. Tidying up the orchards. Cleaning out the chicken pens. Sometimes they cleared the kitchen table and took out thin brushes and jars of water and pots of colour and large sheets of creamy paper. The girl liked this the best. It was a form of story. She imagined a world in her head and then brushed it onto paper. Most times, it didn't match the picture in her mind. But she didn't care.

Once a week they walked the three miles to town. It was a bright and busy place. People moved quickly and made a lot of noise. Leah kept close to her mother and held her hand tightly. She watched people from the corner of her vision. Once or twice someone caught her eye and smiled, but she ducked behind her mother's legs.

Part of her was glad when they made the hot and dusty journey home, their arms clutching brown paper bags filled with groceries. Part of her was sad, but she didn't understand why.

And on Sundays they repeated the journey, this time in their best clothes, which always felt damp against the skin when they arrived in town. They sat in the coolness of the church and listened and prayed.

In the evenings, after dinner, they washed the dishes

together. Sometimes Leah's mother talked of Leah's father. She told tales of a stranger. A young man who had travelled the world in a soldier's uniform and had returned tired and broken. A man who had seen a pretty young woman sitting bolt upright in a church pew, her eyes sparkling with a life that had shrivelled within him. After the service, he had approached her and introduced himself as the man she would marry. Her mother laughed when she told this part. And then she cried. Afterwards she hugged her daughter, dabbed a foamy sud from the sink on the tip of her nose.

'Just you and me, now,' she'd say. 'Just you and me.'

Then Leah watched evening settle over a parched landscape and counted stars as they freckled the night. Sometimes she sat at her mother's side and listened to her read from a thick book. The stories were difficult to understand and she couldn't see the life in them. Then her mother put her in a tub near the fire in the front room, wrapped her in thick towels that smelled of flowers, tucked her into the big bed and read her a fairy story.

After Leah's mother closed the bedroom door, Adam came. Leah lay in the dark and felt him arrive, though she never quite saw the moment he appeared. They talked quietly, though Adam rarely said much. He sat on the end of the bed and listened as the girl wove stories into the dark. She never heard him leave either. But when her mother opened the door later and carried Leah to her own bed, he was always gone.

There was safety in routine. The nights of summer flickered past.

One evening, Leah's mother didn't read her a story at bedtime.

Instead, she lay down next to her. Warm air wrapped itself around them.

'Leah,' said her mother. 'I want to tell you about a special book. You have heard stories from it. Every Sunday, when we go to church and sometimes in the evening. It is not a book you've read by yourself yet, because it's too old for you. But you will. It tells wonderful stories. And it teaches us wonderful things.'

Her mother felt underneath the covers and took her hand.

'This book is about love. And one of the things it teaches us is this: I give away all I have, and if I deliver up my body to be burned, but have not love, I gain nothing.'

The girl liked the music in the words. But they didn't make sense in her head.

'Love never ends,' her mother continued. 'Prophecies will pass away, tongues will cease, and as for knowledge, it will pass away. Now faith, hope and love abide, these three; but the greatest of these is love.'

The girl didn't know what to say, so she said nothing.

'You love me, don't you, my angel?'

She knew the answer to this.

'Yes, Mummy,' she said.

'And I love you too. More than I can say.'

Silence gathered. A swollen moon dusted the room with silver. The girl thought her mother had fallen asleep, but it seemed her voice was only resting.

'Just a little more from this book. It says love does not rejoice at wrongdoing, but rejoices with the truth. Love bears all things, believes all things, hopes all things, endures all things. What this means is that if you love someone you must never tell them lies. Do you understand? I will never lie to you and you must never lie to me. Only then can our love last for always. Do you promise? Do you promise never to lie to me?'

'I promise, Mummy.'

'And I promise, too. We will love each other always. We will not lie.'

Leah's mind circled the world of sleep. She felt its

warmth stealing her thoughts. There was something lurking in her mother's words. A danger, like the shadowy evil in a fairytale forest, but she couldn't pin it down. She recognised the language of fear, though. It filled her mother's voice and made it thick. But she knew she could make it go away. Words were power.

'Yes, Mummy,' she said.

It was easy.

'Sounds like you were happy as a kid,' says the girl.

Once again, I've almost forgotten she is here. My mind freezes around the burning image in my head. A small girl cocooned in love and darkness and stories. I press the pause button of my memories, and it is now, only now with time stilled and mind lucid, that the thought explodes like a soft and soundless bomb. That far away night was the last moment I'd experienced happiness like that.

All those years. All those long and dusty years.

Yes, the worm was in the apple even then. I knew it. But I had hidden the knowledge from myself.

I attempt to focus on the girl's words. They appear

to float, insubstantial. Or do I detect an edge of irony?

'I was happy,' I reply. 'We were happy.'

'That farm you lived on,' says the girl. 'You said there were apple trees. But you must've grown other stuff. Or kept animals. How tough was it, way back then, being a farmer?'

She has not turned off her machine. The red light stares at me, unblinking. This is one of my good days. On other occasions I might not have noticed it. Or noticed how this child is using words designed to nudge me from my course. She is pleased with her linguistic trick. But I am not fooled.

The girl deserves an answer. Or perhaps she doesn't. I give one anyway. This, I know, is the ritual of human interaction. You give. You take. None of it makes much difference.

'The farm was large when my father died. Thereafter, it shrank steadily. Inexorably, looking back on it.'

'So what did you grow?'

'Apples,' I say, and my hands remember their cool hardness. 'After my father died. Just apples.' For a moment, the room fills with the sharp sweetness of their smell. Then it fades and a ghost-odour of disinfectant and fear lingers.

'Were you able to live off just apples?'

'No, which is why the farm shrank. Mother sold off parts of it, year by year. Not much during the Depression, but after. When neighbouring farmers eyed our paddocks, were eager to expand and had the money to do so.' I smile, but keep my lips together. I hate the toothless grins of the old. They make us fools. Or reptiles. 'Mother shaved our land like cheese. A slice here. A slice there. I didn't know when I was a child, but the world was shrinking towards me. The stories I read led me to believe in worlds expanding to infinity. All the time, mine was becoming smaller, circling down onto a patch of apple trees and a girl.'

'Sounds tough.'

I study the girl. We have spent time together and it is courteous to pay attention. She wears denim shorts and sits with her legs crossed under her on the chair. I wonder briefly where the confidence of youth goes. Does it wither with time or flee abruptly one hope-forsaken morning? She wears make-up that is inexpertly applied. Allied with that blue gash in her hair, it gives her a brazen look. She twists the curious metal bar in her eyebrow from time to time. It is a nervous gesture and I feel certain she is unaware of doing it. The tic sits uneasily with her veneer of assurance, hints at complexities beneath the surface. I think she struggles with something.

Every person is a mystery. Most days I accept this. But today, for reasons I cannot fathom, I want to visit the inside of another head, if only briefly. There are stories locked away there and I am lonely.

'Tell me about yourself, Carla,' I say.

She twists her eyebrow stud and smiles, though that twists too.

'It's Carly,' she says. 'And there's nothing to tell. Sixteen. Student. What can I say?' She waits, but I let the silence work. Most people can't live in silence. They have to fill it, even if their filler-words rarely stick.

'What?' She smiles and spreads her arms in appeal.

'Tell me about your family,' I say.

'Oh, them.' Her mouth bows downwards. 'Well, that won't take long. Older brother who is mega smart. Doing medicine at uni. In his third year. Going to specialise in cancer.' She bites her bottom lip. 'Dad is dad. Makes heaps of money from property. He calls himself a developer, but he doesn't actually *build* anything. Just buys and sells. With other people's money. Mum teaches kindy. That's it.'

'And you?' I say.

'Me? Average Year 11 student is all.'

I think about the word 'average'. Is there a story there? The invisible child, hidden behind a sibling's dazzling beam? The father disapproving. He attributes her refusal to shine as wilfulness. The mother resigned, but in the still of night interrogating herself about where she might have gone wrong. I like those characters, but they don't ring true.

'Do you have a beau?' I ask.

She moves her hand to her hair.

'What?'

'A boyfriend.'

'Oh, yeah. Sort of. He goes to the same college as me.'

Her eyes flick away and I read the sign. Her boyfriend is the story. I will tease it out, though it will take time. This girl has to be squeezed like a tube of toothpaste to extract anything.

'What's your boyfriend's name?' I say.

There is the slightest hesitation.

'Josh.'

'And he's a student?'

'Well... not a great student, to be honest. He's a musician. Guitarist.'

How appalling, I think. It's wise to keep this to myself.

'And you're happy together?'

'Oh, yeah. Sure.'

That's a lie. It's in her voice and the way her eyes slide off my face once more. I will let this mature in my head.

'Do you wanna rest now, Mrs C?' she asks, too brightly. 'I don't want to tire you out.' She reaches towards her machine.

'I'm happy to carry on,' I say. She folds her hands together. Is there disappointment in that movement? 'The memories are bright now. Sometimes they dim and I cannot get them to flare. Tomorrow might be one of those times. Where was I?'

The girl sighs. As an exhalation it is almost imperceptible. 'Your mother,' she says. 'How she loved you and how you promised never to lie to each other.'

There is resignation in her voice and I realise where I have been going wrong. My story does not have conflict. Or rather, at the *start* of my story I have not signposted it sufficiently. No one, least of all the young, wants to listen to the emotional soup of simple reminiscence. The human animal craves drama. The warmth of pity. The attraction of evil. The joy of terror. Happiness is, at best, dull. At worst, it's a crime.

'Yes,' I say. 'Love is the finest of all experiences. As a

daughter yourself, you must know the peculiar, intoxi-cating joy of the mother—daughter bond.'

The girl gazes at me blankly.

'But what happens, Carla, when that love turns dark? When you wake one morning and realise your own flesh and blood has become a stranger. What do you do when you find that, in the name of love, the stranger is capable of killing?'

Her finger plucks at her lower lip and I think I have her attention.

CHAPTER 3

O N MY TWELFTH BIRTHDAY, my mother beat me with a leather belt until I bled. Then she locked me in the barn for three days. The same barn my father had used to spread his brains over the walls. The stain was still there seven years later. It was the only thing I had left of him.

It was coincidence that it was my birthday.

It wasn't coincidence that she chose the barn as my prison.

My crime was curiosity. For over five years, my mother had written her book. Three hours a day, six days a week. She didn't write on Sundays or on religious holidays. At the end of each session she shuffled the papers together and placed them in a large box kept in the corner of the kitchen. Then she locked the box with a key she carried on a chain around her neck. I watched the ritual often, through the kitchen window. I still stayed outside while she was writing. Three hours a day, six days a week.

My thirst for stories had not diminished over the years. On the contrary, I had insufficient books to slake that thirst. Mother had a library and I think some of the books in it were my father's. I had read them all, even those I had no chance of understanding. Apart from a small collection of fairy stories, the books weren't for children. There was nothing for a twelve year old girl.

Sometimes, when we walked the three miles into town, I would persuade mother to allow me to visit the store where Mrs Hilson kept a small collection of books among a general clutter of bric-a-brac. There was no library in the town and no bookshop. Those didn't come until thirty years later. Mrs Hilson's collection was a poor substitute, but for a starved girl it appeared a feast of unimaginable richness. We bought a book once a year, for my birthday. I would agonise over my choice for months beforehand. The greatest leaders in history — those who weighed the futures of generations in their hands — did not feel the weight of decision-making as keenly. But despite our being poor customers, Mrs Hilson allowed me to sit in a shadowed corner and read. I think she was lonely and liked the warmth of another presence. Hardly anyone came into her store.

So I stayed for an hour while mother shopped or talked to people from the church. I read what I could, buried myself in words. It was always a surprise when she tapped me on the shoulder for the dusty journey home. Though the clock said sixty minutes had passed, for me it was seconds. A week later I would pick up the story where I had left off. Over the years, I finished many books this way. Piecemeal. A crumb here, a crumb there. And my hunger grew with each small mouthful.

I had not spoken to my mother about her writing since our initial conversation. I understood it was something that would come my way only when she was ready. Yet often my thoughts would turn to the contents of the box. It was, of course, more attractive because of its mystery. And I remembered her words. That she would write a story about a place where we could live forever. I wanted to visit that place so badly that it hurt. Perhaps it was because I had not the smallest clue of where that world was or what riches it might contain.

Curiosity nibbled at me and its teeth were sharp.

One day, mother was talking to a neighbour in our front room after inspecting one of the larger paddocks on the edge of our farm. I could hear the low murmur of voices through thick doors. The man's voice was raised, urgent. My mother's voice was quieter, and although I couldn't detect individual words I could sense the determination in which they were steeped.

The key to the box lay on the windowsill. I caught a flash of light from the corner of my eyes as I walked across the stone flags. It winked at me. I stood, frozen by possibilities.

I was not, by nature, a child susceptible to impulses. Maybe that was because my life did not admit the opportunity to indulge them. The farm was a known place. So was my mother. Everything, with the notable exception of my reading, was ordered, safe and incapable of change. I paced out my childhood along a pre-determined path. The key gleamed with the promise of diversion.

I trembled as I picked it up. I trembled more as I eased it into the lock. I took great care, worried about scratching the casing with inexpert fumbling. Does that show knowledge of wrongdoing? Maybe so. Certainly I knew, though nothing had ever been said, that what I was doing was wrong in my mother's eyes. I listened

The barn was sliced with light. The gaps between boards allowed slivers of sun to highlight dancing dust. During the day, the sun formed narrow spotlights picking out a show that played endlessly.

Mother padlocked the door. She returned four times over the next three days, bringing a jug of musty water and a plate of dense, dry bread. These she placed on the floor and left without a word. I grew to dread the grating of the padlock as it turned in its hasp, the hushed ritual of my offerings being placed before me, the click of the key turning again and the sound of footsteps retreating into silence.

It was *her* silence that scared me most.

On the last visit, her face was shiny with tears. This time, she had nothing in her hand. She weaved over to where I lay as though ill or drunk, though I know she had never touched alcohol in her life. She placed her arms around my neck and drew me towards her. She sobbed into my skin.

'We have sinned,' she said, though her words were difficult to understand, muffled as they were by emotion and my body. 'We have sinned, my baby.'

Afterwards we prayed for hours. We knelt side by side in the barn and let words rise in the air, drift and curl until they dissolved. Our prayers were smoke. Tears ran down my mother's face throughout. After an hour I found my own face wet. We sobbed and prayed, prayed and sobbed until we were cleansed, scrubbed clean. Maybe it was simply exhaustion, but I don't think so. I felt pure as though something dirty or corrupt had been driven from me. My mother and I were charged with love. It spilled over and bound us in soft chains.

'I love you so much, Leah,' said my mother. 'I love you so much.'

'I love you too, Mamma,' I sobbed.

I was as golden as the beams of light which still sliced the air.

Throughout my imprisonment, I heard the snuffling and whining of Pagan, my dog.

Mother wouldn't allow him to be with me, though I didn't ask. It wasn't a situation where I dared ask. He circled outside. Once or twice he tried to dig his way under the wall and I worried mother would find him and punish him. But he finally gave up. Wherever I was in the barn, he would lie down as close as he could to my unseen body and whine gently. I talked to him through the walls and we calmed each other.

Adam was my warmest company throughout the coldest times.

He had changed over seven years. In the early days, he was a fiction drawn from my limited reading of what a brother should be like — incoherent, yet knowledgeable and brave. A visitor from a world that was partly alien and partly familiar. And his role was limited by my needs. He took me to places in my imagination, and when I didn't require him, which was often, he was not there.

Three days in the barn changed all that.

Adam came while I was still sobbing from my beating. He had grown. His hair no longer stuck out at strange angles, but fell in a sleek curtain over brown, almond-shaped eyes. He knelt at my side and lifted my top which had stuck to my wounds with blackened, partly dried blood. I winced as the fabric peeled. When he glimpsed my back, I heard a sharp intake of breath. Then he took off his own shirt and tore long strips from the material. It was almost white, soft as gossamer. Even through the pain and the tears I noticed his body how firm it was, the flatness of his belly. A thin, pale scar snaked along his left side. I saw his form as it would be when sculpted by years to come.

Adam took one of the strips and dipped it in the jug of water. His face was set, lips in a thin and disapproving line. He bathed my wounds one by one with a gentleness at odds with his expression. His touch stung at first. I flinched from contact. But he worked steadily, wringing out the material, dipping into the water, smoothing away the blood and the pain.

'Talk to me,' I said. I was scared of his silence as well.

'What is there to say?' he replied, his eyes never moving from his work, as though he was an artist and my back his canvas.

'She loves me,' I said.

'I can see.'

'No,' I said. 'You can't.'

We said nothing more until he was done. Then he found scraps of material, old sacking that he shook to remove the droppings of rodents and the dried husks of long-dead insects. Adam placed them on the floor and formed a bed fit for a fallen princess. I lay on my stomach, watched the twirl of dust in the bands of light and felt the slicing pain recede. He lay beside me and I buried my fingers in his hair.

'It was my fault,' I whispered.

'No.'

'I pried where I shouldn't have. I sinned. God does not love sinners and I deserve punishment.'

He sighed. His breath was warm on my cheek.

'You seem very sure of the mind of God, Leah. I wouldn't be. Your sin was small, your punishment out of proportion. Love played no part in this. Love does not tear flesh, nor glory in pain.'

I knew how to counter his argument. I had heard it during drowsy mornings in church. I had heard it from my mother. I knew the answer.

'God is love,' I said. 'But God is also vengeance. And that is right. How can we do good if there are no consequences for doing bad? I angered my mother and I angered God. That is why I brought the punishment on myself. If I had avoided sin, I would not have to suffer now.'

There was a long silence.

'God and your mother. Are you sure you aren't confusing the two, Leah?'

I jumped to my feet and the movement brought a fresh wave of pain. I felt skin tearing and I didn't care. I paced through bars of light and shadow. Outside the barn, Pagan whimpered.

'You should go, Adam,' I said, but I didn't look at him. 'I don't want you here anymore.'

And he went. But not before I felt his arms around my neck. He kept his body away from the raw meat of my back. I stiffened with anger, but the touch of his skin on mine was a kiss.

'I love you,' he breathed into my ear. 'And I will be here when you need me.'

Then, nothing. I turned. The barn was empty except for a tangled mat of sacking and the play of light on a dark, fan-shaped stain against weathered wood. Pagan whimpered again and I felt an almost unbearable sense of loss.

'I'm sorry, love, but you really must go. Leah tires easily these days. I'm sure you understand.'

It is my nurse. I say she is my nurse, but of course that is not strictly true. There are dozens of people like me in this Home, and she, along with the other staff, has responsibility for all of us. 'Home' is a word frowned upon by the officials at this institution. Apparently, it has negative connotations. Strange. I always thought home was associated with happiness.

This used to be a home. Now it is a residence. I am impressed with this sign of progress.

Jane, the broad-beamed nurse, she of the flaming hair,

the faint hint of an Irish accent and a husband who is wrong. This is a good day. I often forget her name. I look upon her as mine for reasons I can't properly explain. It's just the way she looks at me, as if she sees a person divorced from the wear and tear of unforgiving years. It is rare, that look. It is precious.

The younger girl startles as if caught in an unspeakable act. She gets to her feet and turns off her machine, slips it into her schoolbag.

'Oh, wow. Sorry. I didn't realise the time.' The words rush from her, a jumble of sound. I wonder if she believes speed of movement and words is atonement for unspecified sins. 'Sorry.'

I don't argue with Jane. She has the vitality of youth with all its unshakable conviction. And to tell the truth, I *am* tired. It is only when I stop talking that I realise how tired.

The girl crouches in front of my chair. She smiles and I'm afforded a close-up of the grill that fences her teeth. I must ask her about that. She rubs my hand and it feels pleasant.

'Bring in a photo of your boyfriend next time,' I say.

'Josh?' she says. 'I've got one on my phone if you're really interested. Hey, I've got dozens.'

She rummages through her bag and pulls out a phone. Her hands dance and soon there is a photograph on the screen, but I have to squint to see it. Of all the symptoms of the body's decay, it is the loss of eyesight I resent most. Hearing is something I can do without most times. Television is better without sound. Deafness spares so much unnecessary pain.

The boyfriend has a lazy smile. He is good-looking, knows it, is relaxed with who he is. He holds a guitar, his head turned slightly towards its neck. There is an abstract design tattooed on his left arm. The boy has a moustache and beard that join to frame his mouth. I think of Spanish conquistadors or Hollywood pirates. He wears his youth with pride. I manage to get him fully in focus when the screen blanks and he is swallowed in darkness.

'You don't have a proper photograph?' I ask.

The girl frowns. 'I might have one in my purse somewhere. A passport photo he didn't need. Hang on a moment.' She unloads her bag, piles up a mass of hair clips, lip gloss, scraps of paper. 'Here we go.'

She hands me a small, dog-eared photograph. It's frayed at the edges. I know how it feels. The boy this time is face-on to the camera. He is serious. It's a photograph the police might take.

'Can I borrow this?' I ask. 'Just until the next time you visit.'

The girl hesitates. She is weighing things. The photograph is personal and she scarcely knows me. But confronting age also makes the withholding of anything a source of guilt. I am harmless and I am old. Denying the elderly makes one feel somehow soiled.

'Sure,' she says, though she doesn't sound it. 'I'll come back tomorrow after school, if you're up for it.'

I feel very good. In my mind, if not in my eyes, everything is sharply focused.

'I suspect I will still be here.'

She turns at the door.

'Hey, Mrs C. You said something about killing.'

'Ah yes,' I say. 'I did. My mother the murderer. It is part of the story and I will get to it. In time.'

She laughs and it is sunshine.

'You're like one of those people who write thrillers. My English teacher is always going on about it,' she says. I almost expect her to wag her finger at me. She doesn't. 'What's it called? A cliffhanger.'

'The hook is always what happens next,' I say. 'The oldest and crudest element of story. But effective. You just need to keep turning my pages, Carla.'

'Carly,' she says.

After she leaves I think about turning pages. The girl has gone to a part of her life that is closed to me. Her family. The brother carrying the burden of extravagant hopes. The father who develops property. What does he look like? I see him as overweight in an expensive suit. He mops his brow constantly with handkerchiefs that his wife irons for him. He is good with computers. She is overweight also, unhappy, tells impossibly cheerful stories to cross-legged children and wonders where the time goes. The girl's parents glory in a shared history and are reconciled to a shared future. It is a burden they both carry. Passion is a memory, dog-eared like the photograph I still hold. There is pleasure in this, creating fiction out of real people's lives.

Death. Yes. There are two deaths to come. And I am responsible for one.

I wonder what the girl would have thought if I'd told her that.

I'm glad I didn't mention it. Sometimes there can be too many cliffhangers. It is so easy for the exhausted reader to slip and fall.

* * *

Dusk comes early or maybe I have lost track of time. Jane says goodnight at the end of her shift, as she always does. Through the darkness-smeared window of the lounge I see her husband waiting in the car. He drums his fingers on the door. His face is in shadow, which suits me. I don't like his face.

'See you tomorrow, Leah,' she says. Her smile looks as if it's been freshly applied. I admire her uncrushable spirit. At the same time, I'm saddened by it. She deserves better than fingers drumming on metal. Good temper can blinker your perception of unhappiness. Or increase your tolerance of it. There's danger in that.

'If God spares me,' I reply.

'Sure, get away with you. You'll outlive us all,' she says, buttoning her coat.

I cannot remember when I heard a prediction so profoundly depressing.

Dinner is awful, as always. Everything is soft. I hate this topsy-turvy childhood, where you shovel in mush at one end and need assistance to get rid of it at the other.

If I were to define the tragedy of age, it would be this: the impossibility of achieving dignity at the very time you are convinced it is the only thing worth saving.

Afterwards I talk to Lucy.

She is my best friend and, unlike me, her mind never wanders. She remembers the name of the current Prime Minister. I forget what we had for breakfast. Lucy has visitors. Her daughter comes once a week and she brings me a present on my birthday and at Christmas. I like her consideration, mainly because it is so unfashionable. Lucy and I sit in too-soft chairs in the residents' lounge, like ancient bookends.

'How are you feeling, Leah?' she asks.

'Sharp as a tack,' I reply. 'It's funny how it goes. I'm like a camera lens being constantly altered. One moment, everything is fuzzy. The next I'm crisp, with amazing depth of field.'

She laughs.

'You've read too many books,' she says. 'Sometimes you use words in ways I can't imagine.'

'You can never read enough books,' I reply. 'It is an enduring loss that my eyes don't allow me to anymore.'

'Well, what about large print editions?'

I snort. 'It's like being shouted at. It gives me a head-ache.'

'There are audio books.'

I wave a hand. We have had this conversation before.

'Audio books don't smell of paper and the sweat of the writer,' I point out. 'Reading is partly the weight of the book in your hand, the feel of a page as you turn it. It is not an experience you can approximate.'

'You *are* sharp tonight, aren't you?' she says.

'I intend to enjoy it while I can.'

We sit in silence for a considerable time. Only friends can do that and not feel uncomfortable.

'Lucy?' I say. She turns her damp eyes to mine and I have the strangest feeling I am looking into a mirror. Her hair is thin and white, like mine. Wisps stick out at odd angles and I know she can do nothing to control this. We have clouds for hair, subject to their own cosmology. Her skin is loose and there are dark circles around her eyes. Her hands are knotted with arthritis. But her eyes. They are what remain of youth, a wet reminder of the way we were.

I realise I have lost the thread of what I wanted to ask. She waits patiently.

'Do you think we would have been friends in the past?' I continue. 'Or is our friendship now just another consequence of ageing? That we share the same space and have no choice.'

She thinks about this. Another thing I admire about

Lucy. She won't give the unconsidered response. She knows I deserve better.

'I don't know,' she says finally. 'Maybe not. Does it matter, Leah?'

'No,' I admit. 'Probably not. It's just that I get strange thoughts, Lucy. I get such strange thoughts.'

She considers me for a moment. 'I told you. You've read too many books.'

Yes. I have read many. My mind drifts and I am reminded again of Adam, how he appeared to me in the barn all those years ago. He wore clothes I had never seen and therefore could not imagine. Adam talked in ways I had never heard. He used words as old as time. How could I have created that? If we spin fiction, we must do so out of materials we have to hand, and my reading then was in its infancy. They were my salad days of literature. Looking back, Adam appears to me now as a transfigured boy from the fiction of the fifties. But when I brought him into being, the words that gave those boys life had not been written.

So how can I explain him?

I have a theory and it is plausible. As far as it goes.

I view the past through the strange kaleidoscope of time and see it distorted, as we all do. Yet I know I was a child driven and derided by loneliness. It is natural to fill our particular vacuums with the stuff of the imagination. I made Adam out of need. I made him well. And he survived, became someone who didn't need my belief to continue his existence. He chose his own path. He was like a child who had grown and taken on his own identity, his own independence, as children must.

Is that possible?

It is a good question.

Increasingly, I believe that when I have poured my story into the child, I will find the answer.

Perhaps.

CHAPTER 4

MY DREAMS ARE THIN.

I see Adam step down from the cross above mother's bed. His forehead is dotted with crimson. The dog. What is the name of the dog? He twitches, then is still. It is an electrical charge. There is a burning smell. Drool, thick as syrup, stains my dress. An apple. Green and polished, reflecting the sky. I have to look closely to spot the worm. It wriggles like my thoughts.

Arms stretched to the side. A diver gathering himself. All the world spins into that moment, the split second before the plunge. A spin of images. The face of a woman. She is dressed in black. Features are sharp, carved by severity. Only the eyes. Only the eyes. Something is there, a memory of what used to be. This woman is everything to me and I am something to her. She fades, churns, becomes lost in the maelstrom.

Faces, places, sounds. Some are now. Some are then. I cannot sift them. One face looms above me. It has red hair and I should know it. I'm sitting in a dusty corner, reading a book. The words don't make sense. That is Mrs Hilson over by the table. She is old. One of us is old. She looks into my eyes and her mouth moves, but if there is sound it is blotted by the air. Red hair. Something snakes from my arm. There is a container above me. Snakes. The garden. Apples. Green and polished, reflecting the sky. I have to look closely to spot the worm. It wriggles like my thoughts. There is a book.

'It's okay, Leah. You're fine.'

Whose are those words? Are they directed at me? Leah. That is my name. I grab hold. My name is a life jacket, or a thin strip of wood afloat on the choppy seas of my mind. I must keep hold. But there is a whirlpool and it sucks me down. I cannot resist it. What is the name of the dog and who is the boy and there is a woman and there are fingers around her throat and she chokes and is afraid ...

* * *

A different woman, with clouds for hair. I lie in a bed and she holds my hand. I think she is my friend. I hear words.

'I am here, Leah.'

'You are going to be fine.'

'Can you tell me my name?'

There is much more. Sometimes I try to reply, but I don't know where words have gone. They are buried and though I search and search they elude me. I think days pass. There is also the woman with red hair. Most of the time I stare at the ceiling. It has stains that make patterns. They appear to be telling me a story, but I can't identify with the characters. I am so tired …

'Do you remember me, Mrs C?'

I have to think for a while, but it comes to me.

'You're Carly,' I say. 'You've been listening to my story.'

She smiles. I remember the bright braces, the flash of blue and the dog-eared photograph. They were part of the cascade and tumble in my mind, but now I separate them, see them in context.

'You had me worried for a while there.'

'You shouldn't worry,' I say. My words are emaciated. While I've been away, everything has lost weight. 'Worry about the living.'

'Hey, Mrs C. Feeling sorry for yourself?' Her voice scolds, but I'm too old to be punished by people anymore. Particularly by a child barely out of the womb.

Memories are a different matter.

I suppose feeling sorry for myself is the way it would sound. But it is not self-pity I feel. It is exhaustion. And something more. Impatience. I am a shadow in the land of the vibrant. Time will not lend me substance. It will relentlessly strip it away. Why? Why bother when what I suffer from cannot be cured, can only degenerate? They say that when you face a momentous journey, the anticipation is worse than the travel itself. That it is better to get it over with.

For once, they do not lie.

'I've been rambling,' I say. The girl doesn't reply, but then it wasn't a question. I've been lost. Now I've returned, but the journey has made both the present and the past vaguely unfamiliar. I'm caught between two worlds and can't fit comfortably in either. 'How long have I been gone?'

She twists the metal in her eyebrow.

'Not sure. I think ... three days.'

'Prop up my pillows, please,' I say. She does and I catch the sharp smell of young flesh. It reminds me of apples and salt water. She offers her arm as I wrestle myself into a more comfortable position. My neck hurts. Most of me hurts. Carly lifts a cup of water to my lips and helps me drink. It softens the sharp edges of my throat.

'Do you want me to continue with the story?' I croak.

'Hey, no. No. I just came in to see how you were getting on. You need your rest, Mrs C.'

I do not want to rest. I tell her so. What I don't tell her are my reasons. One is obvious. My moments of lucidity are becoming fewer and I worry that soon I won't be able to find the words. They'll slip and squirm. Or they'll dance in my head, like motes of dust, and never form pictures. This story needs to be told. It has been buried too long and I think … No. Think is far too strong a word. It is not even a feeling. But I cannot rid myself of this pale belief: that something will be achieved when my story is brought from the dark corners of my mind and placed into another's. Something special.

I also believe something else. That the end of the story will also be my end. As if I have been hanging on to life for this one purpose, that as I turn the last page so I will reach my own blank sheet where all words are spent.

I do not tell the girl this. She wouldn't understand and

it would frighten her. Anyway, she has already sniffed at my self-pity. And I do not want to burden her with the notion that her ears or her blinking machine are signposts to death. Nor would I risk her refusal to listen because of misplaced guilt. Because I know, with illogical logic, that this story must be told.

'Are you sure you're up to it, Leah?'

My nurse is bustling around the bed, tidying, fluffing pillows that don't need fluffing. Her hair is alive against the white walls of my room. It glows like fire. I can't quite place her name. I will later when I have stopped trying. Memories are best approached this way, kept in the furthest reaches of your perception, glimpsed from the corner of your eyes.

'I'm sure,' I say.

My nurse and the girl exchange glances. *What can we do with her?* they seem to say. Then the child with the hidden story takes the machine from her bag, places it on my bedside table. She leans back in her chair, curls her legs beneath her. I lean back into my too-fluffed pillows and close my eyes.

The story takes shape, but I cannot fill the character. The girl I was is far away in time.

CHAPTER 5

THE GIRL KEPT THE boy away for hours.

She fanned the flames of her indignation, made the heat of her anger into a barrier. But all fuel must be consumed and she hadn't the will or energy to replenish it. As day faded into night, he returned and she was glad. They sat side by side against the padlocked barn door, legs stretched out before them. The boy put his arm around her shoulders and drew her close. Outside, the dog whined. She rested her head against the boy and they were silent.

Shadows lengthened and the interior of the barn changed shape. The familiar bulk of a packing case became inked in, forms merged together. Night changed the scene, invested it with mystery, charged it with menace. Her eyes were drawn to the stain on the wood opposite, the site of her father's last thought before explosion and metal blew it out of existence.

What was that thought? Suddenly the girl was filled with a hunger to know. Memories of her father were diluted almost to nothing. She remembered faded nights and a voice that grew from darkness. Faint at first, tapping at the door of sleep, forcing admission. Sitting in bed, a blanket wrapped around her, listening to the discord of words from a buried room. Her father, muttering sounds that refused to resolve into meaning. Except...

From Hell.

From Hell.

A litany that punctuated a rising pitch of agony. And she knew that whatever came from Hell tortured her father in his sleep, pinned him to a sweat-soaked mattress. His words tumbled now, rose in volume, were studded with screams. And her mother. Her mother's voice murmuring comfort, a quiet counterpoint to the crescendo of terror. The girl stared at the void of night, held her blanket closer, waited for Hell to make its final attack, as it always did. Only then would it retreat.

The assault culminated in a scream that chilled her blood and made her flesh crawl. Silence. And then sobs that soaked through walls, her mother's soothing murmurs. Fifteen minutes. Twenty. Until the night absorbed the dying whispers and she lay down, stared through the window, waited for sleep to creep back, reclaim those it had deserted.

From Hell.

The distorting mirror of memory?

Perhaps.

All people were stories. This was something the girl understood. It was the fabric of her world. But for the first time in her short life the girl considered this: that when people were gone, gone too were their narratives. Some ghosts might linger in the memories of those left behind, but they are doomed to further fade in time, as all must fade. Thereafter, nothing. She felt the ache of not knowing. She longed to visit the page of his mind and read the story written there. *A glimpse into his world*, she thought. That would do. That would suffice.

Across the barn, the shadows thickened and swirled and resolved themselves. It was as if the darkness had taken on life. Slowly the stain coagulated, became a man slumped against the back wall. A wedge of blood and brains was a bouquet against seasoned wood. The top of his head was a ruin. For a moment the girl thought she caught a glimpse of the shadowy outline of a rifle cradled in the arms, a faint glint of steel, the stench of dirt and fear.

And then the world dissolved.

A diseased sun bled across a ruined landscape.

The boy and the girl wandered, unseen, through the nightmare.

The earth was churned, reduced to mud as far as the eye could see. Only a few trees remained, but they were husks, all branches stripped bare. Nothing green grew or could grow. The world was grey.

Men lay in a trench cut into the earth. They cradled rifles, heads bowed, muddy water to their knees and waists. Rats scurried through the trenches. A few swam, creating thick ripples. One lifted its muzzle from the chest of a slumped figure, gazed at the girl with blood-red eyes. Its whiskers twitched before it returned to feeding. The girl crouched, ran a hand through the mud. It felt alien, sodden with death and leached of hope.

The boy took her by the hand, drew her to her feet.

Each sense was assailed. The whines and screams of shells tore the air. The stink of blood and despair. And too much, far too much for the eyes to comprehend. A shell landing in a group of soldiers stumbling from the trench. A rain of blood and flesh. One man sprawled in mud, smoking. And then his face gone, brains splashed across those who lay beside him.

The girl tightened her grip on the boy's hand. They trudged down the line, feet sucked by an earth reluctant to release each step. Within the trench, at intervals, were buried chambers. A soldier emerged blinking from one. There was a whistle in his mouth. He waded through mud, gesturing at the slumped forms of men. Most struggled to their feet. A few broken forms did not. The soldiers attached bayonets to the ends of their rifles. They gathered around rickety ladders set against the trench walls. The man blew his whistle.

The boy and the girl were surrounded by a crush of humanity. They scrambled up a ladder and saw no-man's-land laid before them. Craters. Embankments of barbed wire. To left and right a silent tide of men flowed from the trench. Some ran, others walked. But all moved forward. For ten seconds, maybe as many as thirty, the trench oozed with the sound of countless boots sucking against mud. The girl glanced back. More men poured over the top. Hundreds, thousands. And shells falling. Always, the shells falling.

The girl looked for her father. She knew he was there somewhere. But all the men appeared the same. She ran with the tide of soldiers and time froze. Minutes lasted an eternity. Dozens of men surged ahead, their rifles tilted, bayonets forward. Some screamed, though no sound could be heard above the wail of shells and the drumming of enemy fire. Mouths were opened in a ghastly mime of horror or aggression. And then the sound of machine guns. The stench of burning powder. The earth pulled. And the bullets hit.

The boy was at her side. Images tumbled slowly. Men falling in waves. An explosion to the left, then to the right. A soldier tripping over a headless corpse. A body, like a puppet, caught on barbed-wire, twitching. Air tore at her lungs. Blood. Everywhere blood. And bullets. Everywhere the mad whine of bullets.

The girl stopped, put her hands over her ears, closed her eyes. She couldn't hear the sound of her own screaming. The boy held her, rocked her. The world around them continued its descent into madness. And then, after an eternity, the other noises faded, died. Her screams pierced the silence. She opened her eyes.

Nothing stirred within the barn.

The girl dropped her hands to her sides, struggled to

fight the panic. Slowly, her screams diminished, faded to silence. Her throat felt raw, violated. She turned her head, laid it on the boy's chest. He stroked her hair and said nothing.

The night passed. When day arrived, most of the girl had gone. In her place, a young woman lay among the scattered straws of wheat, the droppings of rodents and the slices of sun that picked out a faded stain on weathered wood.

I open my eyes.

Carla ... Carly stares at me. She plucks at her lower lip. The red eye of the machine winks from my bedside table.

'Oh my God,' she says. 'That nightmare. That's horrible.'

'Yes,' I reply. 'I think you'll find that's the nature of nightmares, Carly.'

She winces slightly, as if my words have nicked her. We stare at each other across our own no-man's-land, like enemy soldiers.

'I guess the real question, Mrs C, is whose nightmare was it?' she says.

I wait. The girl is becoming interesting.

'I mean,' she continues, 'you're trying to persuade me that somehow you *lived* an episode in your father's life.'

'Am I? I thought I was telling you a story.'

'It could just be a nightmare, pure and simple.'

'True,' I say. 'But I checked. Much later. I found my father's military history. He *was* there. A place called Fromelles in France.'

'That proves nothing,' she says. Agitation makes the metal in her eyebrow wriggle like a worm.

'Proof?' I wave my hand to dismiss the word. 'Don't worry about proof. The only important thing in a story is truth.'

That makes her brow wrinkle further. The metal bar is beginning to annoy me.

'Fromelles,' I continue. 'From Hell. Appropriate, don't you think? On 19 July 1916 two thousand Australian boys died in fewer than eight hours. I believe I saw a little of what my father witnessed. If you don't, that's your choice. But it explained so much to me. How could anyone get that experience out of their head? Unless — and what an irony this is — a bullet might be the only way of erasing it.'

There is silence for a few moments. I take a glass of

water from the bedside. I am pleased to note my hand does not shake as I raise it and drink. Carly's brow remains folded in a frown. She drops her hands into her lap.

'Another question, Mrs C,' she says. 'Let's say I accept your 'truth'. You wanted to know your father's story. But from what I can tell, you'd have been way better off not knowing it.'

I place the glass carefully back on the cabinet and purse my lips, as if weighing her remark. I don't need to. But pauses are useful sometimes. They can imbue a response with the cast of wisdom.

'What's your view, Carly?' I say. 'Are you glad you heard that story?'

She frowns again.

'Not sure "glad" is the right word. I mean, it's pretty powerful…'

'And your life has been changed, however minutely, in its telling,' I say. 'No. All stories demand to be heard. It is an inextricable part of their nature. It defines them.'

She nods slowly as if I have said something profound. God knows there are few advantages to layered years and senility's lengthening shadow. Issuing statements and having them mistaken for wisdom is one. I relish it while I have the chance.

'You're making me think,' she says. 'Mum and Dad would be amazed.'

I smile and she glances at her watch.

'Hey, better get going.' She kills the blinking light and puts the machine back in her bag. 'I've been here for way too long. Sorry, Mrs C. You must be bugg ... really tired.'

I don't argue. It is not so much physical tiredness, but a weariness of spirit. I am drenched in it.

'Come back tomorrow,' I say. My voice sounds scratchy, thin in my ears. 'I promised you a murder and I always keep my promises.'

'I'll be here.'

'But a story for a story,' I reply. 'Tomorrow you will tell me one of your own.'

'A story, Mrs C? I don't have a story.'

'Yes you do,' I reply. 'You probably just don't know it yet.'

Confusion flutters on her face and then is still. She skips to the door. It is many years since I have been able to move like that. She is a force of nature. All her actions, the very cast of her body sparks with energy.

'Carly?' I say. She stops and turns. 'Don't wear make-up next time you come. And take out that ghastly thing from your forehead. You have a pretty face, and I wonder what it is your make-up is hiding.'

Her hand goes to her cheek. It is impulse. I have been rude and her expression struggles between two conflicting emotions — justifiable anger at my unwarranted insult and unjustifiable respect for brute years. I almost hope she instructs me not to wear my old age so openly, that it suits no one. She opens her mouth and I will the words to spill forth. They don't.

'What I'm hiding? It's called acne, Mrs C,' she says.

Carly grins crookedly and leaves.

Tonight I will talk to Lucy.

Time is running out.

I can feel it.

THE MIDDLE

It's only oblivion, true:
We had it before, but then it was going to end

CHAPTER 6

IT IS A BEAUTIFUL day. A few clouds in a sky as sharp as my mind. It's good to be alive. I feel like the only person who savours this self-evident truth.

Jane comes to me in the morning. Her hair is redder than usual, her smile bigger.

'Leah, my favourite patient! How are you today?'

'I thought you weren't allowed to call me a patient, Jane. Isn't there a rule?'

She hasn't changed into her uniform yet. I like seeing her dressed in normal clothes, even the baggy ones she favours. It's a glimpse into the outside world, a connection somehow. I could almost persuade myself she is my granddaughter.

'Ah, get away with you. Don't you play your word games with me, missy.'

'You are even more cheerful than normal today. Has someone died?'

She smacks my hand, a playful tap.

'It's obvious you're not away with the fairies,' she says. 'Are you going to make this a hard day for me, Leah? Are you going to beat me over the head with your words?'

'Of course not. And as for fairies, we have sworn off each other's company. For a time at least. It's difficult at my age to resist their allure. I'm drawn to their light.'

She sits next to me and takes my hand in hers. Most times I'm embarrassed by the texture of mine. Old, cracked leather. Today, though, the sun is shining and it's good to be alive. I squeeze her hand. It's warm with life.

'I've got news,' she says, and I know what it is. I can feel it in the pulse of blood through her skin. But I almost don't want to hear it.

'You're pregnant,' I say.

'Yes!' Her excitement lights her from within. It shines from every pore. 'And you're the first person to know. After Alan, naturally. But even my mother doesn't know yet.'

It's shameful to admit it, but my first reaction is

dismay. I see again the drumming of impatient fingers on metal, the sidelong glances at other women's legs and a sneer that oozes lust. I am too judgemental. The day is too beautiful. I smile.

'That's wonderful Jane. Congratulations.'

Maybe if she wasn't so wrapped in warmth, she might see the transparent insincerity of my words. But new life is so demanding. It refuses to give up its spotlight. I have seen this in other women.

'Thanks, Leah. I knew you'd be excited for me.'

'How does your husband feel about it? It's a big responsibility being a parent.'

'Alan's thrilled. We've already discussed names.'

But will he be so thrilled with the thickening of his wife's figure, the sleepless nights, the soft chains that bind? I think not. Already he flutters around a range of different lamps. And when the glow of the marital lamp changes direction, when it shines upon another helpless being exclusively, will the pull of the different be too great to resist? People's lives are infused with small, familiar dramas that run continually. I see only a small portion, but even that is too much sometimes. I wonder briefly why I am so concerned with images of light. Perhaps it's because of the sun's blessing.

'We were thinking of Leah,' says Jane. Her eyes are cast downwards. It suits her.

'A problem if it's a boy,' I remark.

She tilts her head and offers a reproachful look.

'Such an old-fashioned name,' I continue. 'She might grow up to resent it.'

'It's not so old-fashioned anymore,' says Jane. 'Biblical names have been popular for years. I like it. Really. And not just because it's your name, though I'm glad it is, but because it feels right. Solid. Anyway, at this stage it's just an option. Mind you, we're struggling for boys' names.'

'Adam,' I say. Jane laughs.

'And that's not old-fashioned?'

'Someone told me — I can't recall who it was now — that biblical names are popular nowadays.'

She looks at me and a cloud of worry sweeps across her face. It is a face ill-suited to wear that emotion and I am both touched and guilty to be the cause.

'I'm joking, dear.'

She smiles and it wipes her face clean.

'Adam?' She rolls the name around her mouth, experimenting with its taste. 'Adam. I like it. Maybe. Why Adam, Leah? Is that someone you knew?'

I gaze out of the window for a few heartbeats. There

are so many responses I could make, but none of them are satisfactory. Each choice burns with inadequacy. And layers and layers of memories...

'Adam was someone I loved,' I reply. It's true, but it does not say enough.

'That's so sweet,' says Jane. She grips my hand tighter. 'What happened to him?'

'He left me,' I reply. 'I made him leave.'

She doesn't say anything else, but sits holding my hand as if it's a lifeline. I watch clouds scud across a powder-blue sky.

'A deal is a deal,' I say. 'A story for a story.'

The girl isn't wearing make-up. I don't know whether to be pleased or disappointed. If she can't stand up to an old woman, albeit a forceful one, what chance does she have with other, more personal pressures? Then again, her eyebrow stud is still there. Conformity and rebellion. An interesting mix. The nakedness of her face is vaguely embarrassing. She seems younger even than her sixteen years. I wonder what I have exposed.

'I don't have one. Seriously,' she says.

'Then I will start,' I reply. 'But you owe me and I will demand payment. Where was I?'

'The barn.'

'Ah. The barn. Yes. I have spent too long there. I have always spent too long there. We must move forward in time. Love awaits us. And murder.'

CHAPTER 7

Mʀ Cᴀᴍᴇʀᴏɴ ᴡᴀs ᴏᴜʀ closest neighbour. He owned a large farm about three miles away. It bordered ours. He was the visitor the day I tried to read my mother's book. The one who invited me over to play with his son.

About a year after the barn incident, mother and I took him up on that invitation, though mother's motives had nothing to do with finding me a companion. I wasn't aware of it at the time, but I think she only went to sign some documents transferring a portion of our land into our neighbour's possession. We didn't do social visits. I don't know why she took me along. Perhaps she didn't trust me to resist the call of the strong box and the story buried within.

We walked. It must have been an odd procession. I was in my long dress, the one reserved for special occasions, like church. It was shapeless and old-fashioned, even for those times. But I wasn't aware of such things. I had very little contact with anyone my own age, so I had no standards by which I could judge myself. Actually, I had very little contact with anyone by then. Mother taught me at home. She considered school a threat to our cocooned existence. I had read of such places — playgrounds washed with laughter, orderly desks with heads bent over slates, the smell of chalk and youth. But for me they remained a bright, inaccessible fiction.

Mother's dress was dark and plain, her hair swept back into a tight bun peppered with grey. The severity with which she kept it brushed back tightened the skin on her face so that she looked faintly yet constantly alarmed. I remember her sharp nose and her firm chin. She was angular and formidable. It was difficult to track changes over time, but I suspect she had become much thinner since my father's death. What happened to the people we once were? Where did that young woman go, the one who smiled from a church pew when a sad soldier told her she was beautiful and that she would marry him? When I think of mother now, I see only her sharp nose, her firm chin, her eyes gleaming with inner resolve, her long, dark clothes that hung like a statement of gloom.

Mother was consumed by her own notion of love, but nothing in her appearance betrayed it.

Pagan shuffled at my side. The years had taken their toll on him. He must have been about twelve or thirteen and had long since ceased to be a working dog. By this time there was scarcely a farm and therefore no work for him to do. He was a border collie and bred for action. I suspect inaction dried him. Or made him transfer his thwarted needs onto me. Every time I stepped out the front door in the morning, he lurched to his feet, tail wagging. From that moment until I went back into the house he was constantly at my side. Even at night he slept as close to my bedroom window as he could. I fell asleep to the sound of his tail beating gently against the verandah.

Adam was the fourth member of our group. He skipped in front, often walking backwards so he could see my face or I could see his. Since the time in the barn he had been like Pagan, an almost constant companion. I never really knew what he would wear from day to day. Sometimes he would be a character from the book I was reading at Mrs Hilson's, particularly if it was a book of which he approved. This day he was resplendent in Lincoln green. I was halfway through a book about Robin Hood and he liked it. We spent happy times in Sherwood Forest. I have said my world was small, and though that is physically true, in my imagination I have travelled through this world and countless others. Adam was by my side every step of the way.

That day he was trying to make me laugh. He would sometimes get a step in front of my mother and make faces at her. There was something absurd in the way her gaze remained fixed on the horizon while Adam put his fingers into the corners of his mouth and made gargoyle faces. I tried to keep a neutral expression, but it was difficult. Then he withdrew an arrow from the quiver on his right shoulder, nocked it and aimed the arrowhead straight at mother's face. I burst out laughing.

Mother stopped and gave me a look one-third curious and two-thirds pained.

'What in the name of God is the matter with you, Leah?' she said.

'Sorry, Mamma,' I replied. It crossed my mind to find a reason for my outburst; perhaps that I had remembered something funny I'd read in a book. But I resisted. Since we had made our pact not to lie to each other, it had assumed the status of a sacred vow. I couldn't lie to mother. I believed what she'd told me, that love and lies could not co-exist. I believe that still.

But that didn't mean I had to give her an explanation for my outburst. If she'd asked me, it would have been a different matter. But she didn't. I was convinced by the logic that says withholding the truth is not the same as lying.

'When we arrive at Mr Cameron's, I want you to be on your best behaviour,' she said. 'You cannot go around giggling like some kind of retarded child. Do you understand?'

'Yes, Mamma,' I said, casting my eyes downward in what I knew was the appropriate expression of contrition. When we started walking again, I gave Adam a vicious stare, but he winked at me. He didn't try to make me laugh again, though.

It was not difficult to know when the boundary of our farm gave way to the boundary of Mr Cameron's. Everywhere on our side were signs of neglect. I remembered a time when father had employed a full-time hand. Then there had been a procession of casual workers, not just fruit pickers, but also shearers and stockmen. But all that changed under my mother's control. The full-time worker was dismissed, the stock sold off, casual workers turned away when they came looking for work. We concentrated on the orchards and the chickens and let the rest revert to nature. We would have starved if mother hadn't sliced up the farm and sold it, paddock by paddock, acre by acre.

Mr Cameron's farm was in good shape. The fences were neat and well-maintained, the paddocks ploughed and tended. His was an oasis that nibbled at the edges of our dust bowl and gradually devoured it.

'Welcome, neighbours,' he said as we approached his house, which was much grander than our humble shack. A woman stood beside him. She was plump and jolly, a caricature of the earthy farmer's wife. There was flour on her hands. Or maybe there wasn't. Sometimes the line between fact and fiction is finely drawn in memory. Or blurred entirely.

The son was also there. I remember him because he appeared exotic. I had seen him before — a number of times in church — but he'd never seemed real. No more than the pews or the lectern or the gold-coloured cross or the cut-out figures mopping perspiration above neck-ties. They were simply fixtures, pinned to one particular scene. Now? Now he was solid. He had an existence outside of one circumscribed place. I felt embarrassed by the blonde hair that fell in ragged lines over his eyes. I was intimidated by the glow of his skin, rich with the sun.

'Leah, meet my son Daniel,' said Mr Cameron.

I had no idea what I was supposed to do, so I did nothing except feign extraordinary interest in the small patch of earth beneath my feet.

'He has a present for you. I remembered that you have a birthday around this time of year. Am I right?'

I nodded. Inside, I was stunned that anyone other than mother would remember. I'd always believed I made no mark upon the world. 'Perhaps you would like to stay out here with Daniel while your mother and I go inside and talk,' he continued. 'Would you like that, Leah? Mrs Cameron will bring you both some lemonade.'

I couldn't recall when so many words had been directed at me by anyone other than Mamma. I tried to find a response, but my brain wouldn't cooperate. I nodded.

'Remember your manners, Leah,' said my mother. 'What do you say?'

'Thank you,' I mumbled.

'Dan,' said Mr Cameron, 'go and get Leah her present. It's on the sideboard in the front room. Then maybe you could take her for a short tour around the farm buildings. Show her the horses.'

'I don't think that will be required,' said mother. Her pinched face seemed at odds with the openness of those around. I felt vaguely ashamed. Of mother. Of me. It was as though we were refugees from another, darker world. A fleeting blight upon this family. 'I would much prefer it if Leah remained on the verandah. We will not be staying long.'

There was silence for a few moments.

'Of course,' said Mr Cameron finally, and if he felt slighted or confused his tone did not betray it. 'Dan, jump to it. I'm sure Leah is anxious to get her present.'

I was. Not so much for the present itself, but because of the experience. I had never received a gift from anyone other than mother. In a predictable world, the prospect of the new was heady. My blood tingled with excitement though I kept my eyes upon the ground.

Daniel disappeared inside the house and returned a few moments later with the gift in his outstretched hand. It had been wrapped, but I knew from its shape and size that it was a book. I almost couldn't bring myself to reach out and take it. All books are cloaked by covers. The story inside this one was doubly concealed, a further layer of bright paper teasing me with possibilities. I felt an almost unbearable sense of anticipation. I didn't want to tear the wrapping paper and reveal its identity.

Even now, I feel the same, that somehow unwrapping a gift destroys a mystery. It is an irrevocable step that dispels magic in the very act of revealing it.

I did unwrap the gift, of course, taking pains not to rip the paper, but gradually unpeeling it. I had a small box under my bed that contained treasures I had accumulated over the years. A pretty stone, a slice of rock with what might have been a fossil pressed onto its surface, a flower carefully preserved between pages. This paper would join the others. It had yellow roses in a repeating pattern. It was a feast to the eyes. Through long and moon-filled nights I would gorge on it.

'It's not new, I'm afraid, dear,' said Mrs Cameron. Her voice was rosy. It danced. 'But I understand you enjoy reading and we have had this for a number of years. To be honest, we are not great readers. I'm pleased it will finally go to someone who might appreciate it.'

The final rose layer revealed red leather binding. The title was embossed in gold onto the leather. I smelled the luxury of binding and paper. The book caressed my hands. It was a copy of *Oliver Twist* by Charles Dickens. I had never heard of the author, but my hands were heavy with the weight of characters and story. I turned to the title page and it whispered in my hand, the paper creamy, soft and rich. I think I stopped breathing.

'What do you say, Leah?' My mother's voice had sharp edges of disapproval.

'Thank you,' I said. 'I love it.' For some reason I could meet the eyes of the others now. Words raced through my head. I was thirteen years old. I was excited. And the words spilled over before I knew it. 'It's the best present I've ever had.'

Mrs Cameron beamed. Mr Cameron smiled. Even Daniel appeared pleased. But mother's expression... I read betrayal there and it stilled the tempest in my mind. Her look sliced to the bone. Words fled. I turned my eyes again to the small patch of earth beneath my feet.

'We mustn't keep you any longer than necessary, Mr Cameron,' said mother. 'Perhaps we could deal with business.'

'Of course, of course.' He ushered mother inside. I was left alone with Daniel on the verandah. Pagan had curled himself into sleep. Adam sat on the railings, legs swinging. He winked at me.

The return journey was quicker. Mother still kept her gaze fixed on the horizon, but there was increased urgency in her paces. The dust puffed clouds around her boots and I had difficulty keeping up. We walked in a bubble of anger.

I said nothing. I wanted to burst that bubble with an apology, but I was too nervous to speak. Pagan fell behind. Adam didn't catch my eye. And the further we walked, the greater the tension grew.

'Did you think I wouldn't notice, Leah? Did you really think that?'

I was relieved she had spoken. Anything was better than her silence dripping with displeasure. But I was also puzzled. I searched for an explanation of her words because I couldn't find a response without one. I knew my words of thanks to the Camerons were a betrayal of all my mother's gifts, that I had diminished her in their utterance. Was that what she meant, that I thought she wouldn't notice the unintentional barbs in my unthinking words? It was the only meaning that made sense.

'I'm sorry, Mamma,' I said, but my apology provoked no response. If anything, her pace picked up, her eyes pinned the horizon with greater determination and the puffs of dust beneath her boots spoke even more eloquently.

'Why are you apologising?' said Adam. His tone was

bitter, as if I had offended him. 'You've done nothing wrong. Why should you apologise?' I couldn't bear the thought I had disappointed him also. I felt overwhelmed with judgement. Its weight crushed me.

'So you are aware of the sin you committed?' my mother added. She still didn't turn her eyes towards me.

There was danger in this. If I was aware of my sins, then it bespoke a deliberate flouting of the moral codes by which we lived. I risked damnation. If I was unaware, then my sin was limited to an inability to think, learn and reflect. This required contrition, but was not damnable in itself. But I knew it was too late for a plea of ignorance. I had already apologised and that confirmed awareness. Anyway, I wouldn't lie to her. I would never lie to her.

'Yes, Mamma,' I said. 'I'm sorry.'

'You spit in the face of our Lord. Our dear Jesus, who lay down his life for you. And this is how you repay Him? This is how you repay me, who loves you as Christ does? An apology is not good enough, Leah. You must burn off the impurities in your soul, you must winnow it of sin, if you are to be worthy of Divine forgiveness.'

Tears burned my cheeks. How had I so offended God? Would He really be angry at the unthinking words of a child? That I loved my gift, that it was the best present I had ever had? I thought of the Fifth Commandment and it was a bright and soundless epiphany. That was my sin. I had dishonoured my mother. Shame welled within, a powerful geyser, an enormous pressure. I tapped, almost gratefully, into something that flooded all my being. I drowned beneath the deluge and gloried in it.

I couldn't speak and that was for the best. Mamma was right. Words were only words. I lifted my eyes to the horizon and saw it swimming through a film of tears. And behind my eyes there materialised an image of Christ's face on the cross and a pain beyond understanding. Not the pain of nails in flesh or the piercing of a lance. That was nothing in comparison to the agony of my betrayal. He loved me. He died for me. And I repaid Him thus.

The sky that blanketed the horizon was bruised and heavy with cloud. Light flickered and pulsed within its darkness. A distant rumble swept over us, followed by another. Pagan whimpered and tucked himself close to my heels. In the gathering gloom, we limped towards the cold of home and the approaching storm.

Mother lit lamps against the dark and the thunder. I shooed chickens into their coop.

Adam watched from a distance. He was no longer

dressed in his absurd costume, but I paid him little attention. He was a shape moving on the periphery of vision, a concern on the border of consciousness. I shooed chickens and prayed for forgiveness with all the energy I could muster. Lightning flickered and crackled in response.

'Leah, this is madness,' he said, once the chickens were in and I was walking back to the house. He kept pace with me and his voice was small. I suddenly understood he was scared. Of what lay within me. 'I see your pain, but I don't understand it. Talk to me. Explain.'

'Leave me alone, Adam.'

'No. I won't. Not until you explain.'

But I didn't. I walked towards the house and my punishment as if to salvation.

Mother met me on the verandah.

'Kneel and pray,' she said. A flash of lightning rolled shadows across her face. I knelt and bowed my head. I caught a glimpse of Pagan lying under the rickety chair. He flinched as another peal of thunder split the air, dropped his head onto his paws and whined. Mother knelt beside me. She held a Bible in her hands. I felt the hard boards under my knees and welcomed them.

'Dear Lord,' she said. Her voice was elevated, rapturous. 'Forgive us our sins, though we are unworthy. And in particular, forgive my daughter, Leah, for her many and manifest failings. Forgive her lustful glances, Lord, for she is heir of flesh and prey to its temptations...'

I was transported as I had been before and would be in the future. Nothing could be compared to stripping bare the soul, the prostration to a power that could cleanse or destroy. It was an experience beyond pleasure and beyond fear. I felt my eyes roll back in my head. My muscles twitched. I was filled with light as surely, as fully, as the storm-charged sky. I teetered on the brink of surrender. But mother's words hooked me from the edge.

'Mamma?' I said.

'...just as Eve, the first and original sinner, the fountainhead of our shame, sinned against your Word. Dear Lord, forgive us now.'

I plucked at her sleeve.

'Mamma?'

She turned her face to mine. It wore a puzzled expression, torn between two worlds. I truly believe she had wholly forgotten my presence, so complete was her communion with the Divine. It was a tribute to my bewilderment that I interrupted her so. Had I been thinking clearly I would never have dared.

'Mamma?' Her form swam before me through a

curtain of tears. I blinked and focused, though my voice was small and lost to my own ears. 'Lustful glances, Mamma? I don't understand.'

I had broken the spell. She gazed at me in a fog of incomprehension for a few moments and her confusion stripped away a layer. I saw, briefly, a scared and fragile woman and my heart clenched. Then her eyes hardened and she jumped to her feet. Her hand plucked at the mane of my hair and she dragged me to mine. I heard Pagan growl, but the noise was swallowed by thunder. It beat a counterpoint to the thudding of my heart.

'Dear God, do you deny it?' she screamed. 'Do you deny it?'

I knew the word 'lust', had read it in the Bible and understood it to be a foul and deadly sin. The word had associations of decay; it conjured an aura of something fetid, like entrails baking in the midday sun. But as to its meaning? It was nothing more to me than patterns on a page and there was a gap in my mind where definitions lived. I was thirteen years old in an age when adulthood lay far off on the horizon of time.

'I saw the way you looked at that boy, the Cameron boy,' mother continued. Her voice was sharp and thin as a blade. 'The lascivious glances, the unashamed desire.

You *must* know, girl, that love of the flesh is base and coarse. It is a mockery of true love, which is spiritual, which is God. It is the reason we were ripped from Grace. It is foul, as Satan is foul. I saw you through the window. I saw the filth and corruption in your face. You are stained by it still. And do you now deny it?'

Mother's hand still gripped my hair, tilted my face towards hers. I could see her eyes, the smooth sweep of her pinned-back hair framed by flickers of lightning. I still didn't understand. Something in the way I looked at Daniel. I searched my memory, but could find no clue. How had I looked at him? He had made me smile once or twice, but that couldn't be it. Could it? But I knew ignorance did not equate to innocence. I *must* have looked upon him in a way that was offensive to mother and to God. That I was unaware showed only a lack of self-knowledge. Nonetheless, I grieved that I did not understand how I had sinned. It meant I could not correct my failings. Contrite though I was, how could I avoid repeating my mistakes? I was terrified that I was set upon a path to damnation and had no means to alter the direction of my footsteps.

'I am sorry, Mamma,' I sobbed. 'I have sinned. Show me how to repent.'

Her eyes softened and the fingers in my hair relaxed. She pressed down on my shoulders and I sank again to my knees. She thrust the Bible into my hands.

'Pray, Leah,' she said. 'Through prayer you will find the way.'

I clasped my palms against the warm cloth of the cover and bent my head over the book. Mamma was right. The book would show me the way. Books had always shown me the way.

I heard Adam's voice, but it seemed a long way off. I concentrated on the words in my head, the recitation of familiar patterns that comforted. Power was invested in words. I knew that even then. Far away, Adam called my name, over and over. I shut him out. I shut everything out.

I do not know how long I prayed. I was suspended in a state of mind where time, too, was suspended. My eyes focused on the arrowhead of my hands, the dark spine of the Book and the knotted boards that flickered as the storm hovered over us. Mother's feet floated into my field of vision. I looked up. She carried another book in her hands. I got to my feet and my knees throbbed with redemption. Mother prised the Bible from my grip and gave me the book. It was my gift. My Dickens.

'Destroy it, Leah,' she whispered. 'Destroy it.'

A deafening clap of thunder filled the silence left by her words. I glanced at the roiling sky, flecked with flashes of light and charged with power. The air tingled, but no rain fell. The world held its breath. I studied the cover of the Camerons' present, the gold stamped into leather, the promise of riches. I opened it. The cream of the paper, the rustle of quality. I took two of the pages between my thumb and forefinger. I tried to tear. My brain sent orders to my body.

But nothing happened.

My knuckles blanched, a muscle twitched in my arm.

But nothing happened.

A tear rolled down my cheek. It hung for a moment on an outcrop of chin and I sensed it fall. In my imagination, I saw a small circle appear on the floor beneath my feet, a dark stain that would, in moments, shrink and vanish.

'I can't Mamma,' I said.

'Nonsense,' said my mother. 'Or do you hold to your sin yet?'

She gripped my hand in hers and yanked downwards. The pages split along the binding, a lightning flash that forked towards the bottom of the spine. It was as though something ripped inside me. My fingers lost their hold and the book fell to the floor. The torn pages drifted after it, like pale memories.

Mother stooped, picked up the book and shredded more pages. There was wild fire in her eyes. In her frenzy she gripped too many and did not have the strength to rip the paper free. She was forced to take a thinner hold. Within minutes the book was reduced to a drift of patterned pages. Some caught in the building wind and danced the air to darkness. Most carpeted the verandah.

Mother panted. Her chest rose and fell. When all the pages had been freed, she tried to split the leather shell, but it was too sturdy. She grunted with the effort. So she cast it from the verandah, a maimed bird that flapped briefly and fell to earth. We gazed at each other. The silence broken only by the wailing of the wind. I dropped to my knees yet again, spread my fingers through the creamy drift of paper.

'Leave it, Leah,' said mother. 'Leave it, as surely as you leave your sin behind.'

I tried to obey, but once more my body rebelled against the commands of the will. I was paralysed. My fingers clenched around a sheaf of paper and I could not prise them loose. Mother grabbed me by the arm and pulled me upright. She tore at the battered prize scrunched in my hands. I cried as her nails tore at my skin, though it was not the physical pain I responded to. Mother screamed into my ear, though the individual words were lost beneath the tide of her anger. I didn't hear the growl until she suddenly stopped and wrenched her eyes from mine.

Pagan was at my feet. Teeth bared, legs tensed, tail tucked between his legs. A small trail of drool hung from his lower lip. He rumbled at my mother. She let go her grip on me and backed away a pace or two. Pagan was rigid with intent.

I do not know if he would have attacked her.

I suspect not.

But in the end it didn't matter. Mother turned to the door, disappeared into the house, returned a minute later with the gun nestled in her arms. Then she took my dog to the barn and put a bullet in his head.

It is strange.

I look back through the pages of my life and some are etched indelibly. I see everything in minute detail, hear sounds that are pitch perfect, smell rain in the air and touch once more the bark of a tree, the rough cast of a dog's coat. But the minutes that preceded the gunshot are cracked and scattered. I know the sequence of events. I understand what happened. But all is fragmented.

Perhaps my mother did not take my dog to the barn at all. Perhaps she made me loop the rope around Pagan's neck, and drag him to the barn. I think I screamed and begged. I think I did not look away when she brought the barrel down. I remember the look in my dog's eyes. I remember the glint of lightning against gun-metal grey. I remember the explosion of sound. I smell still the burning. I remember his legs twitching, stilling with dreadful finality. And I remember the blood staining my dress as I cradled his shattered head in my arms. I looked up once. Adam knelt on the other side of my dog. His face was twisted in pain and love and hatred. He kissed my tears away as quickly as they fell. I held on to my dog and Adam held me.

Outside the sky finally ripped. Rain whipped the ground without mercy.

CHAPTER 8

FOR A MOMENT I have difficulty breaking the chains
of history. I am there, piecing together the frag-
ments of the past. Then I am here and my body aches.
The residents' lounge welcomes with bland familiarity.

'Oh my God,' says Carly. Shock is stamped on her
face. It is naked now there is no make-up to clothe it. I
say nothing.

'Your mother … well, hey, Mrs C, no offence. But she
was a real bitch.'

'Was she?' I reply. 'I suppose it must sound like that.
But she wasn't, you know. She was just … flawed. As
we all are. Some flaws, though, are especially dramatic.
They demand their own spotlight.'

'She killed your dog…'

'And I am the author of this narrative. In its telling, she is not my mother anymore. She has been transfigured into character. I select the words of her portrayal. If she appears a monster, then the fault is mine for I must lack sufficient skill.'

The girl is silent for a moment. I'm not sure she understands my point. That is fine. I'm not convinced I understand it either.

'I mean, I know you loved her and everything,' she says finally. 'At least, that's what you tell me. But she did what she did and *how* you tell it doesn't matter. She doesn't *appear* a monster. She *is* a monster. That's the simple … truth.'

I smile and shift in my seat. Even something as straightforward as that causes pain. My joints have become laced with ground glass.

'This was a farm,' I say. 'A dog was not a pet, but a worker. Mother could have shot him when he no longer had a function to perform. Most farmers at that time would not have hesitated. He ate food we could not afford and gave nothing back. Yet she allowed me to keep him for no other reason than I loved him. Is that the behaviour of a monster or a caring mother? Then he growled, threatened her. She believed he would attack. Every farmer would have done what mother did. The world has changed, Carly. Don't judge the past with the standards of the present. It leads to … error.'

'But …' She stops for a moment, marshals her thoughts. 'You already said it wasn't a farm anymore. Your mum was selling it all off. So that argument doesn't work, does it? And I reckon you know it.'

I smile. I am beginning to like this girl.

'No,' I say. 'You are right.'

She waits and I smile again. I think she is learning my techniques.

'I have had a lifetime to reflect on things that as a child I barely comprehended,' I continue. 'I see it in sharp focus now. Mother was eliminating competition. Now there's a modern strategy for you. When father died, no one remained but me and God. So she poured her energy into both of us. God is a very special friend and I know He's always around when you need him. But he's rather like an imaginary friend, don't you think? Flesh and blood, no matter your spiritual devotion, always takes precedence.'

'What do you mean, "eliminating competition"?'

I take a drink of water. It has a metallic taste. The water of my past was not like this.

'Conflict.' I say. 'My narrative must rely on it, but it is rarely the stuff of day-to-day existence. Mother and I clashed infrequently. When we did it was because someone else intruded on our world, threatened it. The Camerons, later the church. Mother was only truly happy when it was just the three of us. Her, me and God. Alone on the farm.'

'So what're you saying? She got rid of your dog 'cos you loved him when you should have only loved her and God?'

'I don't think it was anything conscious, but yes. Pagan took love that was rightfully hers. When he was no longer there, the last impediment to total devotion was removed. Mother wanted a world that was always shrinking. The farm. Us. Her image of paradise, I imagine, was a small plot of land, a transfigured Eden, containing only her, me and God.'

'Oh, right, Mrs C. Not a bitch, then. Just a freakin' psycho.'

I laugh so hard my water spills. Carly scoops up her recording device and takes some tissues from my bedside table. She mops my lap first, then her machine.

'Judgemental, aren't you?' I say when I get my breath back.

'Hey, I just think some things are right and some are wrong.'

'You'd have got on well with my mother then. That was precisely her philosophy.'

That stops her. She takes her seat again and we are back in the old position. All we need is a television camera and it would be like a political interview where we bat conflicting world views back and forth and no one is any the wiser. She repositions her machine. I wonder who, if anyone, will listen to these hours of rambling reminiscence. It's a strange thought. That when I am dust this device will remain, perhaps in a desk drawer. It will contain the seeds of my story, waiting for someone to water them to life, if they can be bothered, or if time doesn't destroy it. It's an extension. My voice reaching to the future, even if it is destined to be unheard.

'At least you still had Adam,' she says. 'Your mother couldn't touch what was inside your head.'

Carly's voice jolts my thoughts off track. It takes me a few moments to redirect them to her subject. Yet another sign of decay.

'Yes,' I say. 'I still had Adam. But you are wrong if you think he was beyond mother's reach. Oh no. I sometimes think nothing was beyond mother's reach.'

Carly has her legs tucked under her again. It looks painful, but she is clearly comfortable. Her head tilts to one side and she regards me like a bird. I know she wants me to explain, but the time is not right. Anyway, she owes me and it is my turn to collect.

'It's time for your story, now,' I say.

She blinks.

'Hey, Mrs C, I already told you. I don't have a story.'

'You do.'

'I don't.'

We regard each other for a minute or so. I wait for the thumbscrew of silence to produce its effect.

'So what happens now?' she adds. Her hands flutter. 'I keep saying I don't and you keep saying I do? I reckon we'll both get tired of that real soon. Take it from me, Mrs C. Nothing interesting has happened in my life. I can't even remember any stories by other people — you know? The books and stuff we've studied at school.'

'I don't want those. I've probably read them all. I want yours.'

She grabs her hair in her hands.

'Read my lips, Mrs C. I don't have ...'

'Where did you meet that boyfriend of yours? What's his name? Josh?'

She brings one hand back to her lap. The other plucks at her lower lip.

'Josh? At school. I already told you that.'

'Yes, but where specifically? Did you see him in class? Did he sit next to you? What did you think or feel when he touched you for the first time? Was the sun shining or did rain beat a tattoo on tin? Did he smell of fruit or day-old sweat? Are his fingers calloused from the strings of his guitar? Do his hands sing to you? Do they play you?'

Carly laughs. Once again I notice the rainbow of her braces. I will ask her about that when I have extracted what I can of her story. This will be difficult. She resists me. But I will win. Age, for once, is on my side.

'Hey, Mrs C, you sound like my English teacher. She's always going on about stuff like that. Use the senses. Describe the details. Maybe we can come to an arrangement, you and me. What do you charge for writing an English essay?'

I do not reply. She laughs a little while longer, then stops. This time I tilt *my* head to one side. She holds up her hands in surrender.

'Okay, okay. I have no idea why you'd find any of this interesting, but okay. I first saw Josh in the Undercroft. It's a place at my college, close to the canteen, where a lot of students hang out during frees. He was playing his guitar. Something slow. It wasn't fancy. I mean, he wasn't showing off or anything, like some kids do. Like they think they're hot shit and need everybody to know.'

Her eyes become distant. This is what I want. When the vision turns inwards and you lose yourself in a moment. Not recounting the past, but living it. Finding the truth.

'I think that was the thing that made me notice him. The way he was…what's the word? Like, completely living what he was doing. Know what I mean? As if nothing else was happening and nothing else mattered. Into the music. Really into the music.'

'Do you love him?'

Her eyes snap back to the present. I am not unduly worried. She can immerse herself in story and will do so again.

'Hey, Mrs C. That's kind of a personal question.'

'Of course it is,' I reply. 'There's no point asking questions that aren't. Should I waste my time and yours by asking his shoe size? Do you love him?'

She uncurls from her seat and turns off the machine.

'It's time I went,' she says.

'Sit down,' I say. She doesn't. She stands, one hand on

hip and regards me with studied neutrality. Her refusal is a small victory. 'Is this what you think communication is about?' I continue. 'The exchange of trivial detail, the refusal to talk about matters of importance? Words, words, words. They're free. They're easy. They exist, not to reveal the truth but to conceal it.'

I feel a pulse drumming in my temple. This conflict is not what I want, but I am powerless to prevent it. Words tumble through my mind and my lips phrase them. I have no control over this process. There is no filtering of what should be said and what withheld. The girl is offended. She is right to be offended. I am rude. But the words sweep me along. I am adrift on their current. Helpless.

'Say something!' My voice is raised and cracked. 'Your generation … everyone … for years now. Babbling. Always babbling, but saying nothing. Mobile phones. The internet. The communication revolution. It's a cruel joke. No one remembers the purpose of human interaction. The current commerce of words is an insane spending spree and do you know why? Because they are no longer valued. We coin and spend, spend and coin, and among the billions of daily bartered words, the endless babble, the text messages, the gossip in

the newspapers masquerading as news, the verbal diar-
rhoea of television...' The pulse in my head quickens
and jackhammers. 'We say nothing and think we say
everything...'

It is possible I will just talk, let the whole mad sea
flood from me. And a small, buried consciousness within
recognises the irony. This is rant, not communication.
I am guilty of the very thing I rail against. But Carly's
face stops me. There is a film of tears coating her eyes.
They brim, but don't overflow. Her face is set and she
doesn't avoid my gaze.

'I don't want to talk about my feelings, Mrs C. Not
right now.'

I know this is fair. This is reasonable. This is her right.
But my words have an unstoppable momentum. I wonder if I am losing my mind.

'But you expect me to talk about mine, Carly. We have
spent hours together, you and I. I have told you things I
have never told another person. I have stripped myself
bare. Made myself vulnerable to someone a sixth of my
age. I trusted you. I thought we had touched each other
across a chasm of years. And yet you won't trust me.'

She raises her hands and opens her mouth, but I tram-
ple through her attempted interruption.

'Do you think there is any risk in reciprocating, just a little, the confidences I have entrusted to you? Is it that you don't trust me?' She shakes her head as if flinging off annoyance, but I carry on. 'Who am I going to tell, Carly? I am a forgotten person. I will never leave this place. I will be dead soon. Can you not even trust a dead person?'

I have crossed a threshold of good taste and I despise my self-pity even as it makes its appearance. There are tears in my eyes now, but I can't tell from which emotion they spring. I feel them break their banks and flood my face.

'I didn't ask for confidences,' Carly says. Her voice is strong. She wipes her eyes with the back of an impatient hand and shifts her weight to the other leg. 'I came here for research. For my assignment. You said you'd help. I didn't ask for your story.'

'No. You didn't. That was my gift to you. And if you don't value it, then don't come back again.'

There is silence. I am shocked because I didn't know I was going to say that until the words appeared. Now I cannot take them back. Carly stands still for a moment. The dying sun is dipping beneath the trees. Through broad French windows, it paints her red. She hoists her bag upon her shoulder and turns towards the door. This time I want to call her back, but words have dried. She places her hand on the door handle.

'Bye, Mrs C,' she says without turning.

Then she is gone. The door clicks shut.

I sob. I do not understand what I have done or the reasons for it. In all the world there are only two or three people who know I exist, or who would be upset if I ceased to be. And one of them — Jane — is paid for it. How could I offend a child who has spent her precious time — and for the young, all time is precious despite it being in unlimited supply — in listening to the ramblings of an old woman?

My story must be told. And now I have crushed the only medium through which it could be told.

My mind. My mind.

Is it crumbling?

And then, with a power that stops my breath, the answer comes to me.

I am scared.

I am scared to death. Of death. But, most of all, of loneliness.

CHAPTER 9

L UCY AND I SIT in our usual chairs.
Dinner has been and gone and the lounge is empty.
The other residents are in the television room. When I
first arrived here, the lounge was dominated by a huge
television, but I changed all that. There was nowhere,
other than your own room, to enjoy peace, or quiet
conversation. It took considerable effort to have the television relocated. Places like this are resistant to change.

But I am stubborn.

Lucy is like me. She doesn't value noise for its own
sake.

So we sit. Sometimes she reads. Sometimes we talk.
Tonight I need to talk.

'Are you afraid, Lucy?' I say.

'Of what?'

'Dying.'

'Oh, that.'

There is silence for a minute or two. I let it brew. She will answer when she has thought things through.

'Yes,' she says. 'Of course. Aren't we all?'

'Oh, you know. You hear stories of old people who welcome it. Embrace it like a lover. It is these, apparently, who "died as one that had been studied in his death; to throw away the dearest thing he owed, as 'twere a careless trifle."'

Lucy sighs. She reaches across the gap between us and pats me on the arm.

'You know, Leah, just sometimes it would be nice if we *both* spoke English.'

'It *is* English, you ignoramus. By the greatest writer the world has ever known.'

'Catherine Cookson said that?'

I laugh. Lucy does that to me sometimes. It is a great gift, to burst bubbles of pomposity with the blade of humour. I admire it. We sit, wrapped in silence, for a few minutes.

'So are *you* scared of dying, Leah?' she says.

'I am terrified,' I reply. 'And I don't know why. My

body is falling apart and my mind is following suit. I am in pain and it can only get worse. But why should I be scared? There is nothing I can do to ward off death, and anyway, in many ways it will be a blessed release. Yet I know that when the end comes I will struggle for just one more breath. Just one more. I will fight for it to the last of my strength. Isn't that sad? Isn't that pathetic?'

Lucy gets to her feet and struggles to move her chair until she is directly opposite me. I haven't the energy to help her. She sits and now her face is silhouetted against the French window, her hair a dizzying white aura. She takes my hands in hers.

'No. I think it's just the way it is for all of us. It's hard-wired.'

'It's what?'

Lucy smiles. It is a ghostly thread within the darkness of her face.

'It's a term my daughter favours.'

'"Hardwired"? That's ghastly. It makes me sound like a toaster.'

'Your petticoat is showing, Leah. Vocabulary is changing, as the world changes.'

'I wouldn't take much pride in vocabulary that is an affront to good taste. Not all change is good.'

The ghost smile flickers again.

'And what about your God, Leah?' she says. 'Doesn't He make a difference to your feelings about mortality? I would think He should. I mean, what's the point of having a God if it isn't for times such as these?'

I squeeze her hands. She is the closest I have ever had to a friend. Since Adam. The thought is almost too sad to bear. It is a eulogy on my life.

'Oh, God and I have a curious relationship,' I say. 'Sometimes I don't believe in Him and sometimes He doesn't believe in me. It's something we are working through.'

Lucy laughs. 'It's okay to be scared, Leah. It's okay.'

'It will have to be.'

Shadows paint the room. There is a lamp against the darkness, positioned behind Lucy; it bleeds pale light over institutionalised furniture. Somewhere, a clock ticks. Somewhere, a clock is always ticking.

'So do you not believe in God, Lucy?'

She takes her time replying.

'I wouldn't go that far. I think maybe I do. Or perhaps it's as simple as hoping He exists. I was never a great fan of religion, Leah. All that earnestness and ritual. It always seemed like it was trying too hard. Do you know what I mean?'

I do, but I don't say anything. She rubs at her eyes.

'But now,' she continues. 'Now … I don't know. It would be such a waste, wouldn't it? If this was all there is. What would be the point? But, then again, that could simply be wishful thinking, now that time is running out. Maybe life is an exercise in futility. All of it is waste. Truth is, Leah, I don't know. I guess the only certainty is we'll find out.'

She laughs, then continues.

'I used to have conversations like this when I was young. Just after the war, sitting in smoky bars. The meaning of life, the possibility of an existence beyond this one. I suppose, given what we had just lived through, it was understandable. But, God, we were all so earnest, like we were the only ones who'd ever thought such things throughout the course of human history. Such trite things. Predictable and unoriginal. And now, at the end, I come back to the banal. "I don't know. I hope so. Maybe. But maybe not. Toss a coin." I envy you, Leah. I envy your faith, your certainty.'

It isn't that. It isn't that at all. How do I explain? I have lived with God all my years. He was the milk from my mother's breast. Faith and certainty? It was the air I breathed. The root of my being. But dig long enough, mine to the heart of certainty, and there is always a core of doubt, nestling like a stone in the fruit of faith. I have spent years resisting the urge to examine my belief too closely. Because I am scared of what I'll find.

I wonder why I don't tell Lucy my story. Now I have offended Carly, there is a good chance it will remain forever buried. I don't think she will return. Why should she? What profit is there for her? I am old and I am rude. All I have to offer is a story she never wanted. I have nothing she needs. I have nothing she wants.

And then I understand. It is simple.

I cannot tell Lucy because I need my story to live a little while longer. When I die I want it to have an existence beyond me. Lucy cannot offer it time. Carly can. It is her mind that will host it. It will bury itself there and each breath she takes will give it sustenance. Even if the recording fades, if it lies somewhere unregarded, or is broken, Adam and I will live on in memory.

Carly was to be my book.

And I have ripped it to pieces.

History repeats itself.

I am tired and need sleep, a small death at the end of each day's life. Lucy summons Jane, who is on night shift this week. She helps me to my room and prepares me for bed. I used to be ashamed of this help. Now I am too tired even for that.

Carly will not come back.

'Now you sleep well, my dear,' says Jane. She tucks me in. 'Dream of that man of yours. That Adam.'

I do.

CHAPTER 10

THE DREAM IS AS sharp as memory.

It *is* memory.

I pick up Pagan and carry him to the back of the shed. His weight makes the muscles in my arms bunch and cramp, but I do not drop him. The world is made of water. Sometimes, lightning casts everything in silver. The farm is monochrome. My dream is monochrome. Except for the splashes of red that badge my dress and stain my fingers.

I find a shovel from the barn. I dig. Eventually, I tuck my dog down and blanket him with mud. Then I kneel at his sodden grave. Adam wipes my hair from my eyes. He doesn't say anything. I try to pray, but have no words. They stop in my throat. After a while, Adam leaves.

I do not know how much time passes. I am empty

and cannot feel the rain on my skin. Lightning flashes, but I do not really notice. Thunder makes the ground pulse, but I do not really notice. My head is bowed. Time passes.

When Adam puts his hand on my face I turn my eyes to his. He is not wet. His hair shines, even in the darkness, as do his eyes. They flash silver in the storm.

'Come see, Leah,' he says.

'What?' I say.

'Come see.'

He takes me by the hand and raises me to my feet. He twines his fingers inside mine, leads me from the grave. I follow.

Inside the barn, the air is solid. It smells of rain and death. Adam leads me through the darkness. We stop just beyond the hulks of old farm machinery, rusted mementoes of a dying era. Though the dark is hard against the eyes, I see pale patches on the floor.

They are lined in rows, ghostly rectangles. I kneel on the floor and bend towards them. Pages. Curled and damp. Hundreds of them, some in soggy clumps. Others fluttering limply at their edges, stirred by the storm.

'I collected them,' says Adam. He kneels beside me. 'I don't know if I got them all. Probably not. The wind was vicious. Still is. You wouldn't believe how far some of them had flown. I found one or two at the edges of the orchard. Soaking wet. I...'

I touch him on the arm, though I don't look up from the drift of paper before me. He stops talking. My mind is in a strange place. It wrestles with the image of a dog, a blinding flash of light and the smell of burning death. Yet it also considers the pages laid before me, the jumble of story, wet and curled. There is a beginning here. It snakes with the promise of vitality from an ending. Life comes from death. One story ends and another begins. It is too much to reflect on and I am too young. I touch a sheet. The tip of my finger tingles.

There is another small explosion of light on the edge of my vision.

Adam has found my secret store of candles. They were tucked beneath sacking, a few stubs of cold wax, a half-empty box of matches and a chipped saucer. The flame writhes against the draughts, battles against the night. It steadies and when it does, the darkness has been pushed back a few meagre centimetres. It is enough.

Print marches across white space. Words resolve themselves.

'I know I found the opening page,' says Adam. 'It's

here somewhere.' He searches through the mottled pages, gently lifts a sheet to avoid damaging it, puts it carefully back on the barn floor, picks his way through a carpet of story, wary where he places his feet. He mutters in disappointment, continues his search. I reach out and take a page — any page — from the pile before me. The candle's flame swirls and the print dances from light to shadow. When it rests, I read.

The evening arrived; the boys took their places. The master, in his cook's uniform, stationed himself at the copper; his pauper assistants ranged themselves behind him; the gruel was served out; and a long grace was said over the short commons. The gruel disappeared; the boys whispered each other, and winked at Oliver; while his next neighbours nudged him. Child as he was, he was desperate with hunger, and reckless with misery. He rose from the table; and advancing to the master, basin and spoon in hand, said: somewhat alarmed at his own temerity:

'Please, sir, I want some more.'

The master was a fat, healthy man; but he turned very pale. He gazed in stupefied astonishment on the small rebel for some seconds, and then clung for support to the copper. The assistants were paralysed with wonder; the boys with fear.

'What!' said the master at length, in a faint voice.

'Please, sir,' replied Oliver, 'I want some more.'

The master aimed a blow at Oliver's head with the ladle; pinioned him in his arms; and shrieked aloud for the beadle.

The board were sitting in solemn conclave, when Mr. Bumble rushed into the room in great excitement, and addressing the gentleman in the high chair, said,

'Mr. Limbkins, I beg your pardon, sir! Oliver Twist has asked for more!'

There was a general start. Horror was depicted on every countenance.

'For more!' said Mr. Limbkins. 'Compose yourself, Bumble, and answer me distinctly. Do I understand that he asked for more, after he had eaten the supper allotted by the dietary?'

'He did, sir,' replied Bumble.

'That boy will be hung,' said the gentleman in the white waistcoat. 'I know that boy will be hung.'

Nobody controverted the prophetic gentleman's opinion. An animated discussion took place. Oliver was ordered into instant confinement; and a bill was

next morning pasted on the outside of the gate, offer-
ing a reward of five pounds to anybody who would
take Oliver Twist off the hands of the parish. In other
words, five pounds and Oliver Twist were offered to
any man or woman who wanted an apprentice to any
trade, business, or calling.

'I never was more convinced of anything in my
life,' said the gentleman in the white waistcoat, as he
knocked at the gate and read the bill next morning:
'I never was more convinced of anything in my life, than
I am that that boy will come to be hung.'

I lower the page.

The boy was reckless with misery. He was reckless with misery before asking for more. I want to know why. I want to know the history. And the prophecy. The boy will be hung. It is an arrow to the future, sharp and pointed in its urgency. I must know Oliver. I must walk at his side.

'Got it!' says Adam. He steps into my circle of light, a page in his hand. He presses it on me, an offering, a gift. His face is lit, not just by the wash of candlelight, but also by his smile. He glows from within.

I take the page and study it. It is damp. Water stains

are forming. It looks diseased and old. But the words survive. I place it carefully away from the others. I do not even have to speak. Adam knows. I stand and we move among the piles, searching for order.

It takes many hours and all my remaining candle stubs, but we succeed. At some stage the storm passes. At some point the night passes. When the book is complete, dawn is struggling through the walls of the barn. Birds sing in the new beginning.

Pages 221 to 234 are missing. I never find them. Though I read the book many times over the years, in many different editions, I resisted the urge to fill that gap. Always I would skip those fourteen pages.

I am too tired to start reading and I am old enough to know the miracle of story is now fixed. It is asleep and waiting for my eyes to kiss it to life, like all those stories from my childhood. I am asleep as well, curled on the floor in Adam's arms. He strokes my face and I feel the warmth of his body as a blanket.

My last thought is a strange one.

I don't think of Pagan. I don't think of mother, alone in her gloomy bedroom, watched over by a grim God. I don't even think of Oliver and his reckless misery.

I think of Adam, insubstantial as a dream.

And I ponder how something that exists only in my imagination can radiate heat and stroke my face and pick up pages from a torn book. My dog is dead and gone. He is no longer of this world. But at the moment of his death something else has stirred and come to life. Adam is here. Really here.

CHAPTER 11

I WAKE AT TWO-THIRTY FIVE and I know.

There is a moon outside and the walls of my room are painted in silver. The colours merge with my dream. It is not uncommon to wake in the early hours of the morning. Pain is often my alarm clock.

This time, though, my body is at peace. It is my mind that hurts.

I know.

I cradle the knowledge through the long hours to dawn.

* * *

Jane takes my hand.

'It was peaceful, Leah. I promise you that. She didn't suffer. Just went to sleep and didn't wake. I am so sorry. I know you were close.'

There are tears in her eyes. I wonder how she copes with looking after the elderly. Death comes with the job. What effect does that have over time? The constant erosion of emotions by the battering waves of death. The accepted wisdom is that nurses become immune. It is their only defence. But Jane is different. I am glad she is different. When we lose the ability to care we become less than human. But the toll ...

I nod. I have had a number of dark hours to think it through. I do not know how I knew. It is a mystery, and the older I get the more the mysteries accumulate. I no longer try to fathom them.

Lucy was here and now she is gone. It is as unexpected as it is expected.

We talked last night about the final journey. I thought I would be the first of us to set out into the unknown. I was wrong. I wonder if she has her answers now.

'Thank you,' I say to Jane. I rub her hand. It is my office to comfort her. 'We are old. It happens. It must happen. You cannot take it to heart. It's not personal.'

She smiles, but it is a weak and helpless thing.

'Not sure how much more personal it can get,' she says.

'It's not personal,' I repeat.

'Would you like me to stay with you today?' she asks.

'You have work to do.'

I see her mind considering. Her mouth moves to utter the words, but she stops herself in time. *This* is *work. The comforting of the elderly at times of bereavement is what, among other things, I am paid to do.*

'It can be arranged,' she says finally.

'You go about your work,' I say. 'I'm fine. But thank you.'

'I'll get you dressed and into the lounge.'

'If it's all the same to you, I'd prefer to stay in bed. I'm tired, Jane. It wasn't a good night.'

She eyes me. There is doubt there. I shouldn't be left alone to mope. She has a duty of care. For Jane it's not just a statement in a job description. It's a moral imperative.

'What about your visitor? That young lass who comes every day? Do you want me to tell her to come back another time or do you want the company?'

'Send her to my room,' I say.

Jane kisses me on the cheek. I *know* that is not in the care-of-geriatrics manual.

'I'm so glad she visits, Leah,' she says. 'It's put a glow in your cheek and a spring in your step.'

I smile.

'She's a nice girl. I enjoy her company.'

I do not add that I have treated her badly, that in so doing I have probably forfeited the pleasure of her company. And it is pleasure. She is not simply a receptacle for my story. She is a human being and must, therefore, be treasured.

I watch the day grow old and die.

Carly doesn't come.

She doesn't come the next day either.

CHAPTER 12

I AM LOWERED INTO A wheelchair for the journey to
the car. Someone lifts me into the back seat of a long,
black, sleek vehicle. A nurse — not Jane — sits in the
back with me. Our driver wears a dark cap and a sombre
expression.

Despite the circumstances, I am glad when we leave
the Home behind. I cannot remember the last time I left
the grounds. The sun dominates a cloudless sky. I want
to wind down the car window. It operates with a button
and it takes time to work out how to do it. I breathe in
air that is pungent with life and watch the landscape roll
past. My nurse doesn't say anything. I do not know if
that is consideration or indifference, but I am grateful.

The church is small and crowded. I am helped into the

wheelchair once more and wheeled down the central aisle to take my place at the front and to one side. I have the best view in the house. Lucy's daughter kneels before me and we whisper routine sentiments. There is sadness in her eyes, but I think I also detect the faintest hint of relief. I understand that. I respect that.

The minister is young and talks too long. He makes the mistake of assuming a knowledge he doesn't possess. I am faintly irritated by his insistence on appropriating Lucy for God's benefit. I remember some of her last words to me. That organised religion is too in love with ritual. I wonder if he uses the same format for each funeral, the same pious assumptions of a meaning behind all this. It is, I know, in the nature of things. Wheel one in, dispose of it, work through the list. Next, please.

Yet I also know he believes everything he says. His words are steeped in sincerity. It makes forgiveness easy.

I gaze around the church. It is wonderful and if God is anywhere He is here. The stained-glass windows are delicate, exquisite. The pulpit is elegant, the cross simple. No body crowned in thorns and slumped in the agony of victory. A plain wooden cross. Mother would have disapproved. She craved drama in her religion. She expected it to be full of pain. She always had difficulty getting beyond the Old Testament. The New, for her, was like a re-make of an old classic film. It lacked style and tried too hard to please.

The coffin is simple, too. I think Lucy would have liked it.

Once the ceremony is over I am wheeled back to the car. Lucy's daughter has invited me to her house for sausage rolls, curled sandwiches and pointless reminiscence. I have declined. I have said my goodbye. Nothing else remains.

The chauffeur stubs out a cigarette and straightens his cap as we approach. I wonder if he ever thinks about the day he will be driven in his turn, that final crunch of rubber on some gravel-strewn path. Sooner than he thinks if he keeps up the smoking.

My nurse applies the brakes as the chauffeur moves to open the back door. I am touched on the arm. When I turn the sun is directly in my eyes and I have to squint at the figure above me.

'Hey, Mrs C.'

'Carly,' I say. My heart jumps. 'What are you doing here?'

She kneels down into the shade of the car. I see her through the watery film of sun-bludgeoned eyes. She smiles and I am thrilled to see the artist's palette of her teeth.

'I went to the Home,' she says. 'They told me you were here. That it was a funeral. My boyfriend, Josh, drove me.' She points to an old, rusted car at the far reaches of the car park. A young man stands, leaning against the passenger door. He has his arms folded. Even at a distance and even with my failing eyes I can see the boy from the photograph, which, I realise, I still have. One leg is bent. Carly gives him a wave, but he doesn't respond.

'I don't understand,' I say. 'Why the rush? You could have waited until I got back. Or you could have returned tomorrow.'

Carly blushes and then I realise.

'You thought it was mine, didn't you?' I say. 'They didn't tell you I was just a spectator.'

She spreads her arms.

'Hey, you know. I got confused. They said "funeral" and I just made assumptions. It was dumb. I know that. But I asked where it was and they gave me the address. I rang Josh. Here we are.'

I laugh.

'It's okay,' I say. 'I'm surprised it's not mine, as well.'

She laughs too.

I want to apologise, but maybe it's the sun. Maybe it's the silent nurse and the grim-faced chauffeur who smells of smoke. Maybe it's just not the right time.

'I love your teeth,' I say instead. 'They are an explosion of colour.' Her hand automatically goes to her mouth, but she quickly drops it. 'Is that something you chose or something the dentist made you wear?'

'The orthodontist? No. I chose these colours. If you've got to wear braces, well, I figured you might as well go all the way. Know what I mean? Loud and proud. To hell with it. In your face.'

'You made the right choice,' I say. 'They are bright and cheerful. They match your personality.'

The nurse coughs and I battle the urge to stay here talking a while longer just to spite her. She is on duty. Her time is much more disposable than mine. But I don't. Years of submission to duty win out once more. I can't change this. I have stopped trying.

'I am delighted to see you, Carly.' I say. 'I wasn't sure if I would.'

'Ah, no worries, Mrs C. It's just that I've been kinda, you know, busy the last week. Assignments and stuff.'

I think it is a lie. But a sweet one.

'So, can I come and see you again?' she says. 'You know, if you want.'

'That would be wonderful,' I say. 'When?'

She scratches her nose.

'I guess you wouldn't want me to come later today, would you? I mean, this kinda thing probably takes it out of you.' She waves her arms to encompass the immediate environment. The gesture takes in the funeral.

'I would love that. And please thank your young man for driving you here. It was kind of him.'

She glances over at her boyfriend. He has not moved a muscle.

'Sure,' she says. 'Well, catchya later then, Mrs C. Cool wheels, by the way.'

The chauffeur has opened the back door and the nurse is itching to get me out of the wheelchair. I allow myself another sentence. *To hell with it*, I think.

'Thanks,' I say. 'As wheels go, they are certainly ... cool.'

The return journey seems much shorter. I think about Carly talking to the receptionist at the Home and the confusion she must have felt. I know she always gets the bus when she comes to see me. It's something she mentioned. When she thought I was dead, she rang her boyfriend, made him collect her. I can't imagine he was happy to drop everything for an old woman he doesn't even know. He doesn't look like someone easily coerced. Yet she insisted.

I am touched.

She wanted to be at my funeral. She wanted to say goodbye.

I am moved beyond anything I've experienced lately. The tears that stubbornly refused to materialise at Lucy's funeral now make an abrupt appearance. I watch the landscape through their haze.

I am an old fool and I don't know why I am weeping.

CHAPTER 13

Dickensian London was a squalid, crowded, noisy, smelly place.

The author's words were strange. Many I did not understand. But the pictures he painted with them were vivid. Oliver was painfully thin. His spirit shone through his skin. Fagin was not, as he seemed to become later, when the novel was turned into an entertainment for the eyes only, a lovable scallywag, but a bent and bitter soul with darkness in his heart. The Artful Dodger was old beyond his years. He was the sin of the times, a childhood withered before it had had the chance to bloom.

I read to Adam, but in my mind Pagan was always there, his tail thumping on the barn floor, raising small clouds of dust. I finished the first day of Oliver's arrival in London. When I glanced up from the page, Adam was regarding me as if nothing else existed. Maybe it didn't.

'I have seen that place,' he said.

'Show me?' I said.

'So your mother let you keep the ripped-up book?' says Carly. 'That's kind of out of character.'

'It was never mentioned again,' I reply. 'Something changed the day she killed my dog. She never apologised. As I told you before, there was nothing to apologise for. But you don't spend your entire life weighing up moral consequences, as mother did, without wondering if what you did was wrong, if she had in some way betrayed me. So she ignored the issue. I kept the loose pages of my book in an old box in the barn. She knew they were there. But neither of us spoke of it. We carried on as if nothing had happened, our respective secrets in respective boxes. We never mentioned Pagan again either.'

'All that secrecy and fear. It must have been a horrible life.'

'But it wasn't, Carly. Seriously. Mother loved me. I loved her. We both loved the farm.'

She snorts.

'Why do you find that so hard to believe?' I ask.

'You're kiddin' me, right? Unless it's like that battered wife thing. You know, the women who are so low on self-esteem that they end up thinking violence is a kind of love.'

'Listen,' I say. 'I am using the tools of narrative. I am focusing on only part of the picture, the conflict that drives my story. I might have told you instead about the time Mamma dressed us up as characters from a book. She took the role of the wicked witch and I was Snow White, but we laughed so much we couldn't stay in character. Or the picnics by the dam, my head resting on her stomach as I watched clouds drift. Or collecting windfalls from the orchard, the two of us dunking for apples as they bobbed in a water trough. Mamma and me. Soaked in water and laughter.'

The images are sharp in my mind. Every detail is in focus.

The girl doesn't appear convinced. She scratches at her forehead.

'I guess I'll have to take your word for it,' she says. 'Tell me about Adam instead.'

Carly hadn't turned on the recording machine until

I'd insisted. We both knew our talks would never see the light of day in any school assignment. But I wanted to feel my words weren't just fluttering in the air for a while before shrivelling and dying, like moths around an indifferent flame. The machine was a comfort.

'Tell you about Adam?' I said. 'The problem is knowing when to stop...'

I think... It is difficult to know what I think. Even more difficult to know what I believed then, so many years ago. Five lifetimes for someone of your age. But I believe that, at first, Adam changed according to my needs. His personality, but also his looks. Whatever my child-like imagination created as the exotic, the exciting, from the little I knew and the lot I had read. He was *my* fiction.

That changed the night Pagan died. Adam was truly outside of me now. He no longer owed me his existence. And that was wonderful, because he became more magnificent than I *could* imagine. Those eyes, a romantic brown at first, became flecked with grey. His body was no longer the hard and muscled fantasy of a pre-pubescent girl. Not that I had fantasies. Not consciously at least. And I certainly had no conception of sexuality. That was not something taught in church, and, as you can imagine, it was not a topic Mother would have found suitable for instruction or after-dinner conversation. But a sexual nature there was, though I would never have known where it came from nor recognised its manifestations. I think maybe that was part of it. Bury sexuality and it must surface somewhere. For me, it surfaced in Adam. Anyway, he became softer. His hair curled, turned coarser. He wasn't an idealised version of an older brother or a romantic lover. He was ... He was Adam.

And he loved me. I knew that. Perhaps at first he had no choice. I'd designed it as the cornerstone of his creation. But now ... he was freed from that compulsion. He chose to love me. And that made the love sweeter than I can describe.

He was truly independent of me. Adam had little in the way of a sense of humour. He was so earnest, he would take things literally. And no woman I know would create someone with a stunted sense of humour. It's what women find most attractive, or so I'm told. Yet Adam rarely laughed. Even his smiles were, more often than not, a response to mine. He went to extravagant lengths to please me. Some of the places we visited — the landscape of books I so adored — were, for him, unexciting, even tedious. Yet he was with me every step of the way. He grew to hate London in the nineteenth century. The sweaty bulk of humanity offended his soul. Yet he never complained. He knew that for me the world was inside my head. He wanted to be wherever I was.

On the farm, he sensed those few occasions when I wanted to be alone. I'm not sure he understood them. He seemed to think any time spent apart from me was wasted. Yet he would vanish when I wanted to roam the orchards by myself and obviously any time when mother was around. Every morning when I woke he would be curled up at the end of my bed. I once called him as faithful as a dog with a dog's sleeping habits. He didn't smile. He didn't take offence. It was simply what he wanted to do.

And Adam was affectionate. He loved to touch me, the feel of my hair on his fingers or the taste of my skin on his lips. Sometimes we would hug and feel the beating of each other's heart. Even now, after all the long years we have been apart, I feel his absence as a physical sensation. It is a knife within my flesh. It is a knife within my soul.

Carly plucks at her lower lip. I realise she finds it hard to believe. I am slumped in my chair and I know what she sees. An old woman, with hair as dry and dead as parched grass, her skin loose on her bones, crumpled, desiccated, hollow. What would such a creature know about passion? More importantly, why would she have the bad manners to comment on it? It is an offence to good taste.

Yet nothing in her eyes betrays such thoughts. She is absorbed. Maybe moved.

'What happened to Adam, Mrs C?' she says. 'Where did he go?'

'His story is not yet told,' I say. 'We will get there, Carly. You know what they say. All things come to those who wait.'

'I thought it was good things come to those who wait.'

'And do you believe that, Carly?'

She considers this for a few moments.

'I don't know. I haven't had to do much waiting.'

'I have.' I smile.

'Well, what about your mother's book, then?' she asks. 'The one she spent all her time writing. Did you ever get to read it? Or is that something else you'll tell me when the time is right?'

'Oh, I read it,' I reply. 'But not until she died. Apart from what little remained of the farm and some furniture fit only for Mrs Hilson's junk shop, it was all she left me. I remember opening the box, a few months after she died. The key was lost, so I had to force the lock. That struck me as fitting, somehow. She tried to keep her secret right to the end. And beyond.'

'What was it like?'

I travel back to that moment. I feel again the icy hardness of the strong box, hear the crack as the lock yields. The pages are a solid block. I pull them out and place them on the kitchen floor. Hundreds and hundreds and hundreds of them, covered in mother's small, neat script. Her life's work, heavy with responsibility. Words from decades earlier ring in my mind: *I will write a story that will be perfect, about a place where we will want to live forever.* I am scared. But I read anyway.

'It was rubbish,' I say. 'Rambling thoughts, ill-conceived ideas about a way of living that, unsurprisingly, was based upon fundamentalist Christian philosophy. There were rudiments of plotting. Many characters who shared two basic characteristics: all unbelievable and poorly drawn. Maidens whose only distinguishing feature was their allegiance to chastity and virtue. Heroes who were diluted Christs. Villains who were flimsy variations of the Devil. How can you make the Devil flimsy?

It was rubbish, pure and simple. If there was nothing else to make you pity that woman, it was the reading of her life's work.'

'Did you read it all?'

'I tried. It has become a habit of mine to read every book through to its end. I work on the principle that a writer has taken considerable effort to write the words and not to follow the path he or she has laid is, in some ways, a betrayal. But mother's book … it was unreadable. I abandoned it after five hundred pages, a quarter of the way through.'

'What happened to it?'

I raise myself up in bed. My muscles are aching and there is a tingling down my left arm. It is strange. The longer I spend in the past, the fainter becomes the pain of the present. Story as painkiller. When Carly isn't here, all the frailties of my body clamour for attention. Now I find it easy to push the aches to one side.

'I still have it,' I reply. 'How could I not? And not just because it would be cruel to dispose of something that was the product of so many thousands of hours of labour. In many ways, it *is* my mother. Passionate, unyielding in its conviction, sharp, hard and wholly lacking in subtlety. But, threaded throughout, almost undetectable at times, is a seam of love. Real love, not the transfigured, other-worldly love of the spirit, but the kind that has its source in the pulsing of blood that manifests as flushed skin.'

My voice trails away. I see an image, a familiar image. I look through a dusty window at the blurred form of my mother bent over the kitchen table, her hand moving steadily, relentlessly across a page. Her brows are furrowed. The eyes of a child look upon her as a living mystery, a puzzle that *could* be solved if only one found the key. And then, suddenly, the child experiences an epiphany. It's not, as most epiphanies are, profound, but it explodes like a star. There is a person in there, in the moving arm, the crook of the neck, the fixed stare of piercing eyes. And a mother is only a small part of that person. There are hopes, dreams and ambitions. They may be alien to the child. They *are* alien to the child. But for all the harshness and severity, there is someone trapped in that body. And that someone is small, alone and scared.

It makes it easier to love. It makes it impossible not to love.

'It's time to take up my story again,' I say.

CHAPTER 14

About a year after Pagan died, we walked to church on yet another hot, dusty Sunday.

Mother, as always, strode with purpose, the hem of her black dress swinging in the humid air. I walked twenty metres behind with Adam. Occasionally, I glanced back. There were three sets of footprints in the dirt road, though any observer would have noticed only two people travelling through the landscape. If that observer had come closer he would have been disconcerted, possibly terrified, to see a set of footprints appear as if by magic, spreading in sequence across the earth. I worried that mother would notice. But mother never looked back. Never. It was a matter of pride with her. Her eyes were always fixed on her destination, be it literal or metaphorical. And she didn't appear to notice when we returned a few hours later. Sometimes a breeze would obscure the prints or other travellers would disturb the trail. Even so, I tried to make Adam walk on the edge of the track where his footprints were less likely to appear. But he always returned to my side after a few minutes. He just forgot.

When we arrived in town I knew something was different, though nothing appeared out of the ordinary. I understood that was an advantage of routine. When it was broken, however subtly, it screamed for attention. I gazed at the usual groups of worshippers making their way to church. They seemed as normal, but I sensed small changes in the way they held themselves slightly more erect, the way their steps seemed almost imperceptibly more determined. And when I noticed that, I noticed also a change in mother's bearing. She was more charged than normal.

Something was going to happen.

I understood when we approached the church. I had sent Adam away as I always did when other people were around. I was keen to lessen the chances of his detection. He would wait outside the church until the service had finished. Afterwards, mother would talk to some of the congregation before we started the long walk home. Only when we became lone travellers once again on the dusty track would he fall in step beside me.

So mother and I walked into the church alone.

A new pastor stood at the entrance, greeting his flock as they filed in.

This was inconceivable. Nothing changed in town. Nothing. There were deaths, of course. And births. And very occasionally, someone would move away for reasons I never understood. Only later did I see this as the inevitable ebb of people from the country to the city, from poverty to the promise of riches, from dull routine to the illusion of excitement.

A new pastor.

The old one had been a hook-nosed person of advanced years. He reminded me of a crow in his sleek black robes and his sharp predatory eyes. Solemnity was a word that might have been coined for him. He rarely smiled, as if pleasure in the world was something of suspicious provenance, that a smile might lead to a laugh and a laugh to … God knows what. It was better not to take the risk. His sermons were like him. Dark, humourless and solid.

The new pastor was much younger, about my mother's age. He had a small moustache and neat hair. He was good-looking. Even at that age, I knew it. And he was smiling as we stepped closer. My blood tingled with the excitement of the new, the unpredictable.

'Good morning,' he said, extending his hand towards my mother. 'It is lovely to see you here.'

'Thank you, Pastor,' said my mother, shaking his hand. She smiled in turn. 'Welcome to your new church.'

'And who is this?' he said, crouching down so his eyes were on a level with mine. 'How are you, young lady?' His smile broadened. His teeth were very white.

I didn't know what to say. The old pastor had never spoken to me in all the years I had attended his church. He paid no attention to the young. They were below the level of his gaze and he was content for them to stay there. And now this new man not only acknowledged my existence, but expected communication. My tongue froze to the roof of my mouth. I nodded. And then I blushed. If he thought this an inadequate response to his question he didn't show it. He touched my shoulder with a slender finger and continued to smile. I was hypnotised by his expanse of teeth.

'Well, I am delighted you are here today. My name is Michael Bauer, but please call me Michael.'

'Thank you, Pastor Bauer,' said mother. She introduced

both of us and we slipped into the cool darkness of the church. Others were queuing behind us, waiting their turn to be greeted. I liked him. I liked that he'd talked to me. The church seemed brighter somehow. And warmer, as if it had absorbed something of his smile.

Mother did not share my view. That was apparent in the way she sat in our usual pew, the way her head bent in prayer, the way her hands clenched each other. She radiated disapproval. We sat in a cloud of cold distaste.

Most of the service was as normal. We sang. We prayed. But the sermon was different. Very different.

Pastor Bauer stepped to the pulpit, which had been stripped of the gold paraphernalia we were accustomed to. The huge gilt lectern that carried the Bible had been in the form of a massive bird — an eagle, I'd always supposed — and I had quite liked it. On drowsy Sundays I'd occasionally imagined it taking flight, with me on its back hanging on to feathers for grim death as it swooped over strange lands. Now it was gone. In its place was a plain wooden block. Other furnishings had disappeared too. Nothing sparkled. It was almost as though some of the spirit had left the place. But, strangely, I liked the new arrangement. It seemed homely. I breathed easier.

The pastor gazed at the congregation for a few

moments. His smile was permanent. A few people coughed. Somewhere at the back a baby cried and then stilled.

'Good morning,' he said. 'As you will have noticed, I've made a few changes to the interior of our church. Now, no one could call me a professional decorator...' He paused for a moment as if waiting for laughter, but it didn't materialise '...yet it struck me that this house of God was sorely in need of a small spring clean. A little simplification. You may wonder why and, hopefully, in this, my first sermon, I will explain.'

He did. He talked about Christ and the moneylenders. He talked about wealth as something that was of the spirit. He mentioned the Gates of Heaven, a camel and the eye of a needle. Mother, perched on the pew at my side, stiffened with every passing word. I relaxed with every passing word. I understood Pastor Bauer. He talked about love and kindness and charity and simplicity. And he spoke as if he were talking to us as individuals, in language we knew, in language we used in the world outside. His voice did not ring, as his hook-nosed predecessor's had, with anger and violence and retribution.

He did not mention Hell once.

At the end of the service, he stood at the entrance offering a personal farewell to each member of the congregation. Mother strode past him. She was coiled with energy and anger. In thirty minutes I trailed her by a hundred metres. She brought up clouds of dust with each determined footstep. At least it gave me an opportunity to talk to Adam.

'What's got into the old buzzard?' he said.

'Adam,' I hissed. 'Don't talk of Mamma that way.'

We walked in silence for a few minutes.

'She's angry,' I said.

'She's always angry.'

'That's not true.'

'It's nearly true.'

It was, but I said nothing. We followed her along the track. She was like a force of nature, a small dust-devil, a pocket of pent-up energy searching for release.

Later, we prayed on the verandah for two hours. Mother muttered to God throughout.

I caught the word 'temptation' a good many times. 'Pride' also featured prominently.

Later, in my own bed, with Adam curled up at its foot, I puzzled over the source of Mother's anger. I didn't make progress, but I knew something, maybe everything, had changed.

I didn't know it, but my world was about to contract yet again.

'So,' says Carly. 'She didn't like the new guy, huh?'

I have to wrench myself from the past. It is becoming more and more difficult to do so.

'I'm sorry, Carly?' I say. 'I was miles away.'

'I said your mum hated the new vicar, or whatever you called him.'

I laugh. 'Oh, no, dear. I don't think she hated him. Quite the reverse.'

She spreads her arms wide. It's a "please explain" gesture. I am learning this new language of the young. It's direct and it lacks elegance, but economy seems to be a motivating factor. I suppose it has advantages.

'The new Pastor was in his thirties. He was attractive. He was approachable. He had energy, a new way of looking at things. He smiled. Can't you work it out yourself?'

Carly bites her lower lip again and curls one bare foot beneath her bottom. The metal stud in her eyebrow wriggles as she furrows her brow. Then it stills and her mouth forms an exaggerated O.

'You are kiddin' me!' she says. 'You don't mean ... no. You're joking. Oh. My. God.' She bursts out laughing. I find a smile on my own lips.

'Look, I don't know,' I say. 'Obviously, this is not something we would ever have discussed. And it's only a theory I developed years later. But you remember I talked about repressed sexuality earlier? Well, why should mother be immune to that most fundamental of human urges? She had been a widow for nearly eight years. We didn't have guests. The only men mother ever saw were members of the church. Married men. Farmers she conducted business with. Why shouldn't she experience ... lust?'

Carly screams with laughter. She bends over in her chair. Her hair swings below her knees, curtains her face. Then she rises up again, her mouth a riot of colour. I laugh myself. It is impossible to resist.

After a couple of minutes she calms down, presses a hand to her chest.

'Sorry, Mrs C. No offence, but I can't quite see this psycho, bible-bashing fruitcake getting the hots for anyone. I mean ... she was *horny*!'

The thought sets her off again. I should laugh more. It makes me feel young again.

'Call me Leah,' I say. 'I think you've earned it.'

I wait until we have both recovered some control.

'It's only amateur psychology,' I continue. 'And if mother *was* attracted to the new Pastor, how would she cope with that? It would run counter to everything her moral code dictated. Everything the Bible taught her. Lust? Lust was a one-way ticket to Hell. Non-negotiable. So what could she do? Face the prospect of everlasting damnation or bury the emotion beneath a stronger, more acceptable emotion? Anger. Suitably Old Testament. So she persuaded herself that Pastor Bauer was worthy of hatred. He didn't preach damnation. He preached salvation. He preached love. There was a danger in that. He upset her world. He had to be defeated.'

'Jeez! That is seriously fu ... weird, Mrs C.'

We contemplate the state of weirdness for a minute or two before Carly glances at her watch.

'Hey, Mrs C. I should get going. I didn't realise the time.'

'Leah. Remember?'

'Sure. Leah.'

She says the word, but it obviously feels strange in her

mouth. She uncurls herself from the chair and turns off her machine, tucks it into her backpack.

'And Carly?' I say. She turns to me. 'I'm sorry about what I said to you a few days ago. I was rude and nosy. You are perfectly entitled to keep your private life to yourself. It was unforgivable of me. Are we still friends?'

She grins.

'Sure, Mrs ... Leah. And, anyway, I thought about what you said. About what's important between people? And once I got past your grumpiness — again no offence — I reckoned you were right. I'd like to talk to you about the important things. If that's, you know, okay.'

'I'd be honoured.'

She is slightly embarrassed now. She kicks at one shoe with the other.

'Catch ya tomorrow, then.'

'I have a gift for you,' I say.

'A gift?'

'Well, I'm not sure if you'll consider it much of a gift. It's not valuable. In fact, you probably won't want it all.'

'Boy, you're giving this a big build-up, Mrs C.'

'There is a box on the floor of that wardrobe over there. Could you get it for me, please?'

She opens the wardrobe door and rummages around

for a moment. The box must be heavier than I remember because she grunts under its weight. But she drags it out, lifts it onto the mattress next to me.

'Open it,' I say.

She sits at my side and removes the lid. There is a silence while she examines the contents.

'It's my copy of *Oliver Twist* by Charles Dickens,' I say. 'I would really like you to have it.'

'Thanks, Mrs … Leah. Cool. It's kinda … well, buggered.' She brings out the first page. It is leprous with water-stains. I remember when I first saw it. The creamy whiteness of the paper, the crispness of the print. It had passed from youth to age in one stormy night. Now I have caught up with it.

'It has sentimental value for me,' I say. 'And I couldn't bear it if it was just thrown out after I die. It would be a great kindness if you would give it a home.'

'This is the book you read to Adam? When he'd take you into the world you were reading about?'

'Yes.'

'The actual book. Cool.' She turns the page over. 'I'll keep it always, Leah.'

'Thank you.'

She puts the page back, replaces the lid and tucks the box under an arm.

'See ya tomorrow, then.'

'Carly?'

She turns.

'I'm curious,' I say. 'Do you believe in Adam? Do you believe he was real?'

She chews her bottom lip as she considers.

'Sure,' she says. 'I don't have a problem with that.' She grins. 'To be honest, Mrs C, the one I have difficulty believing in is your mum.'

I watch the door for a while after she has gone.

I skip dinner. It is fish and mashed potatoes tonight. I am not hungry and I can't stand the texture. I remember crisp apples. The sound when my teeth pierced the skin and the gush of juice on my lips. Like almost everything else, it is in the past.

CHAPTER 15

I BELIEVE LUCY VISITS ME in the night.

She is insubstantial as a thought. I wake. Or perhaps I don't. The darkness is grainy. My eyes feel coated. Something peels when I open them.

I feel a pressure on my bed, nothing more. A shadow brushes my arm. It could be an affectionate hand. There is a slow exhalation somewhere. It sounds like 'Leah'. For a moment, fear is there as well. But then it clears. I experience a movement in the air, a gathering of something that stirs the hairs on my forearm. A shift in the darkness. The bed moves beneath me.

Then she is gone. Somewhere a clock ticks. Night

sounds settle. I am alone, but something, something remains. It coats the air. It settles on the room, like dust.

It could be happiness.

Jane takes me outside after breakfast. I avoid the lounge now. It is too empty.

The day is clear and blue again. It used to be that the everlasting skies of summer were restricted to memory only, a fiction penned to make the past more vibrant and the present less so. Yet I cannot remember a summer like this. It is perfection born over, again and again.

Jane wheels me down towards the ornamental pond in the centre of the grounds. There used to be a fountain that played at its centre, but it has long since been turned off. I worry about the future. It has no green promise. Jane applies the brakes next to a bench and sits on it, to my left. The bench was a donation from a past guest. There is a plaque that notes the details. I suppose it is a nice gesture, but it's not something I have put into my will. The idea is that the plaque ought to be a testimonial, a physical reminder of a life spent. For some reason, it feels the opposite to me. It is just a plaque. It is just a bench.

'Do you think about Lucy?' says Jane.

She means do I mope about her, have I lost the will to carry on. But she deserves credit in refusing to avoid the subject.

'Yes,' I reply.

'And how are you coping?'

'As we all must.'

'It's the part of the job I really, really hate.'

I study the surface of the pond. Lily pads ride the gentle swells, bright green and polished to an impossible shine. The breeze hints of the sea, far to the south. This is a good place to be.

'You'd be slightly strange if it was a part you enjoyed, don't you think?'

Jane laughs. She holds my hand.

'And what about you?' I continue. 'How's that baby you are carrying?'

She places a hand upon her belly. It is instinctive. It must be hard-wired into the maternal psyche.

'The baby's good. That's what my doctor tells me. But *I'm* not. Morning sickness, Leah. Actually, that's not right. For me, it's morning, afternoon and night sickness.'

'That's a shame. I understand that some women manage to avoid it completely.'

'Yeah. Apparently, I'm not some women.'

'And do you have any pica? I knew someone who virtually lived on vegemite and strawberry jam. Together.'

'Pica?' She wags a finger at me. 'Is there any word you *don't* know the meaning of? But no. No cravings. Well, apart from any kind of food. I'm starving all the time, Leah. It's crazy. Sometimes I just want to stick my face into my meal and *inhale* it. Alan calls me a pig.'

He would, I think. His wife is changing and it won't please him. He is the type of person who must effect all changes himself. He is the sun and everything revolves around him. Now there is a new centre for Jane. That small clump of tissue, nestled snug within her depths, is growing, growing and calling, calling. Beyond his reach and power. He watches the changes and feels small. He would call her a pig. And worse as time moves on and the gravity of the new life swells, deepens and becomes a tug more impossible to resist with each passing second.

'What do they say? Eating for two?' I reply.

'Two? I'm eating for ten. Oh God, Leah. What will become of my figure? I'm already a dress size up. At this rate I'll need a hammock for my boobs. And what if I don't lose it afterwards? Some women take a long time to recover from childbirth. I don't want to waddle around like a walrus for years.'

'You'll be fine,' I say, without conviction.

'Alan is working late a lot recently,' she says after a long silence. I wonder how her mind has moved to this new topic, though the pathway is perhaps not difficult to plot.

'Is he?'

We sit and watch the surface of the pond. I think about the obvious — the cycle of death and birth, Lucy's death and Jane's baby, the endless dance of renewal. I do not know what occupies Jane's thoughts but I suspect it has to do with the warmth of an ember within and the coldness of eyes across a dinner table.

'Hey, Mrs C. Hi! How are you?'

Carly runs across the grass towards me. She waves a hand above her head and her backpack joggles on her shoulder. I feel light-headed just seeing her. *Youth is wasted on the young,* they say. They lie. It fits her contours perfectly. Better than a glove. I want to wave back, but by the time my body has obeyed my brain's instructions, she has collapsed in a heap on the grass at my feet.

'Hey, Leah. Mrs C. Got a proposition for you!' She is excited and in her excitement forgets her manners. She sees Jane and blushes. 'Oh, hi. Sorry. Am I interrupting?'

'Not at all, not at all,' says Jane. 'In fact, I should

probably get along, leave you girls to chat. Do you want me to wheel you back, Leah?'

'Oh, can I?' says Carly. 'Please. Please? If that's okay with you, Leah?'

'Don't fight over me,' I say. 'It's a burden being so popular.'

Carly springs to her feet. She is so energetic it makes me tired.

'Let's stay here for a while,' I say before she can grab the handles of my wheelchair. 'It's such a lovely day and I want to enjoy the sun on my face.'

'I'll leave the two of you to it,' says Jane. 'Not too long, though, Leah. I don't want you dehydrated.'

'If I shrivel any more, I'll be indistinguishable from a prune,' I say. 'Don't worry. Carly here will water me.'

I hear the faint tread of soft shoes on grass. They are quickly swallowed by silence. Carly sits at my feet, cross-legged. She tears up blades of grass and scatters them to the wind. Her face is open. Life has not yet scored it with lines.

'The proposition,' she says. 'Wanna hear it?'

'I'm listening.'

'Do you want to come for dinner tomorrow night? It's Sunday and Mum always does a big roast dinner. You know, chicken, stuffing and vegies. Roasties. I've already asked her and she says it would be great to have you over. Dad's keen, too. I've told them heaps about you, Leah. They really wanna meet you.'

'Dinner? Well, I'm not sure about that Carly, though it's a lovely offer.'

'Aw, come on, Mrs C.' She screws her face up in frustration. 'Live a little. Mum says she'll pick you up and bring you back. I mean, it is okay for you to leave here for a bit, isn't it?'

Gulag Geriatrica. Barbed wire on the perimeter, rott-weilers, armed guards in towers, searchlights picking out the occasional old person in her Zimmer frame tottering towards freedom. I like the image. It makes me smile.

'Yes,' I say. 'We can leave.'

'Then do it. Please? Pretty please. Pretty please with sugar on top.'

I think. She is too young to consider all the implications. Her mind and her body are synchronised. Everything works as it should. What does she know about the unpredictability of bladders? I decide to spare her the details. Jane could help, anyway. There are … devices. Insurance. Though, as with any type of insurance, there is never any guarantee it'll pay out when you need it.

I am unaccustomed to making decisions.

This is a pity. Decision-making is evidence of life.

'You're not thinking of adopting me, are you, Carly? A sort of rent-a-great-grandma?' *At least you'd be able to return me when you get bored*, I think. *The real thing normally comes with a guilt-tag.*

'Tcha!' She waves the comment away. 'It'll be fun. And you need to get out more. When was the last time you went anywhere? When it didn't have something to do with someone dying?'

I don't even want to think about the answer to that.

'Are you sure your parents don't mind?'

'I'm sure.'

'Then thank you. I'd be delighted to come.'

I feel almost dizzy with the notion that I've made a decision, that in a few words I've broken what appeared to be the unbreakable destiny of routine. Sunday night is hard-boiled potatoes studded with dark eyes, and meat fried to leather. It will be a relief to miss that as well.

'Yay!' Carly punches the air. For a moment I think she is going to spring to her feet and embrace me. She doesn't. 'Fantastic. Mum and I will pick you up at five o'clock. We'll eat early. I figured you probably wouldn't want to party most of the night.'

'Want to. Able to. The distinction is a form of tragedy.'

'That is so cool you are coming, Mrs C. After dinner, you could tell me more of your story. It'll be fun to hear it somewhere different, you know?'

'We are approaching the end. I see it in the distance, looming larger with every sentence.'

'Tell me some now.'

'You are anxious to find out what happens to Adam?'

She shrugs. 'Sure.'

'Then I have not been a total failure as a story-teller.'

I, too, am anxious for the end, though I suspect my reasons are different. The sun has ducked among the branches of a tree. It transforms them into a lattice of brilliance. The pond shimmers, reflects flashes of light. The air drones with the language of insects.

CHAPTER 16

THE NEXT SUNDAY I put on my best dress and waited for Mamma on the verandah.

The paint was peeling from the house in great flakes. It was decaying before my eyes. Or shedding its skin. Perhaps beneath the old exterior something new was struggling to emerge. Something bright and shiny.

Mamma opened the door and stepped outside. She carried her Bible. Everything was as it should be. I took a pace towards the rickety steps that led to bare earth before her voice stopped me.

'We are not going to that church today, Leah.'

For a moment I wondered if I had got the day wrong. But that was absurd. It was Sunday. On Sunday, at seven-thirty in the morning, we started our walk to church. Always. Not doing so was as unimaginable as the sun not rising or the dark refusing to gather. I turned towards mother. She brushed a hand through my hair and smiled.

'Church is not just a building, my baby,' she said. 'I've explained this before. It is a state of mind, a willingness to open yourself up to God. And we can do that anywhere. This farm is a church, this verandah. *You* are a church, Leah, and so am I.'

I had heard the idea before, but that didn't make it easier to grasp. If that was so, why had we gone to the church in town in the past? Every Sunday. Never before had mother suggested we worship elsewhere.

'So today, Leah, we will have our own service. Just the three of us in this church of our verandah. You, me and God. How does that sound, my baby? Would you enjoy that?'

I wouldn't, but I didn't dare express the thought. I nodded.

'Good,' said Mamma. 'We will sing and pray and I shall conduct the sermon. It will be just like always. But better. Because we will have God to ourselves. We won't have to share Him.'

* * *

In the afternoon I lay in the orchard with Adam.

By this time, I had discovered Shakespeare. I'd found a dog-eared copy of the complete works tucked away in a corner of Mrs Hilson's shop. At first it had been daunting. The histories, in particular, were very difficult to understand. Almost instinctively, I gravitated towards the tragedies, though there were still many parts of those that remained locked outside my comprehension.

I had no copy of the text with me, but I told Adam the story of *Othello*. As always he listened intently. When I'd finished, he stared at me.

'Aren't you going to say it?' I said when the silence had stretched to breaking point.

'What?'

'That you've seen that place.'

'I haven't.'

This was the second revelation of the day. I felt there was nothing I could trust any longer.

'What do you mean?'

'I mean I haven't seen it.'

I wondered for a few moments if he was angry with me. It had happened in the past, particularly when he felt I allowed Mother to dominate me too much. But there was nothing in his eyes except puzzlement. He picked a blade of grass and split it along the spine with a fingernail.

'It's you, Leah,' he said. 'It is you who sees these places. In your head. Because of the words you read. And when you read them to me, then I see them. And I can take you there. But this...' He threw away the shredded blade. 'This is just what people say to each other. I can see the people. I just can't see the place.'

I didn't read drama to Adam after that. Many years later, when I went to my first theatre and saw Shakespeare on the stage, I was overcome with sadness. The seat next to me was occupied by a stranger. Three-quarters of the way through the production I was assailed by a longing so intense it made me gasp. I needed Adam there, so he could, with me, visit a land the dialogue could not reveal. I wanted him to lean across and whisper to me, '*Now* I've seen the place.'

But Adam was long gone by then. And the man sitting next to me sniffed throughout.

Mother was on the verandah when I returned. She had the shotgun nestled in her arms. My heart hammered in my chest. It was the first time I'd seen the gun since that stormy night.

'What is it, Mamma?' I said.

Mother scanned the ground before our house. She glanced up at my approach, but didn't reply. Instead, she continued to examine the dusty track, occasionally lifting her eyes to peer towards the horizon.

'Have you seen anyone, Leah?' she said finally.

'Mamma?'

'A stranger? Someone on our farm.'

'No, Mamma.'

Adam wasn't a stranger. I did not lie. But I knew this was about him.

'Someone has been snooping around,' she said. She gestured at the dirt with the barrel of the gun. 'Left footprints.'

'Are you sure, Mamma?'

'Of course I'm sure, Leah. We do not have visitors. So who could have left these?' She crouched by a set of Adam's prints. They were clear, the outline of his toes distinct in the red dirt. I said nothing.

Mother stood and squinted against the rays of the dying sun. The barrel of the gun rested comfortably in the crook of her arm, but her finger was curled around the trigger.

'Keep an eye out, my angel,' she said. 'We must be vigilant.'

Adam didn't stay in my room that night. I felt so alone, I cried myself to sleep.

Three weeks later, I found myself trailing behind Mother on the track to town. It was seven-thirty on a Sunday morning.

I had no idea why we were going to church, but I assumed that must be where we were headed. Mother carried her Bible. She walked so briskly I had to scamper to keep within twenty metres of her. Adam flanked us, a considerable distance to my left. I'd wanted him to stay home, but he'd refused. Once again, mother kept her eyes fixed firmly on the horizon. She said nothing to me the entire trip.

The pastor was at the church door, greeting his congregation. His smile was as broad as I remembered it. Mother attempted to walk straight past him, but he partially blocked the entrance.

'Good morning, Leah,' he said. 'And welcome back. How are you this fine day?'

This time, I was prepared for conversation.

'Good. Thank you, Pastor,' I said.

Mother withered me with a glance. I had no idea what I'd done to deserve it.

'Am I right in thinking you brought a companion with you?' the pastor continued. He glanced over my shoulder and I froze.

'You are not,' said Mother. Her voice was ice.

'Ah, I must be mistaken.'

Mother took me by the hand and pulled me into the dark recesses of the church. Her fingers trembled against mine. I could sense something violent rising within her flesh.

'The man is mad,' she muttered.

We took our seats in our usual pew. I wanted to ask why we were here, when the verandah had been our church for the last couple of Sundays. But the trembling in my mother's hand was a warning. I bent my head and prayed, and waited for the storm I knew was coming.

Throughout the prayers and hymns, Mother was her normal enthusiastic self. Her voice was the loudest while we were all singing, though it was far from the most melodic. She couldn't carry a tune, but she made up for her musical deficiencies through sheer volume. It used to embarrass me. Now it was simply another patina in the gloss of routine.

I became tense when Pastor Bauer ascended the pulpit. My tension mirrored my mother's. I felt her become more rigid, as if she was merging with the hardness of the pew. I wondered if those around us could sense the electricity she was generating.

The pastor swept his smile around the congregation, like a lighthouse that bestowed its beam on all. He started with a couple of anecdotes about town life. They were warm and affectionate and anchored firmly in the commonplace. Sermons weren't supposed to be like this. They weren't sermons unless we felt discomfort and guilt, if we weren't squirming against the unforgiving wood beneath. I was accustomed to feeling I had offended God in ways I hadn't understood. Pastor Bauer made me feel like God had a sense of humour. I was confused.

Mother stood when the pastor moved on to the main point of his sermon, which appeared to be about not judging those whose opinions you do not share. He stopped in mid-sentence as he observed my mother's figure, a lone upright among the crowd. Mother said nothing. She simply stood there. I felt her hand reach for mine, clasp my fingers and tug. I stood also, my heart thumping. The eyes of the congregation turned towards us. For a few moments there was silence as the world focused on us.

'Do you wish to say something?' the pastor asked. His smile had reappeared, as if this interruption was not a gash in routine, but something to be welcomed and embraced.

'I do,' said Mother.

Someone coughed. I heard the scrape of leather against floorboards. The church held its breath.

'Then please share it with us.'

'This service is an abomination. You rub salt in the wounds of our dear Saviour,' said Mother. Her voice was low, but I could sense the troubled well of emotion beneath its surface. I stopped breathing. There was a snigger from the back of the church, quickly stifled.

The pastor's smile twisted a little, guttered like a candle flame, then surged back, steadied.

'That is quite a claim, Mrs ...' He stumbled as he tried to recollect our family name. 'Mrs Cartwright. I confess I fail to see how my words have offended Christ. Perhaps you could explain?'

'You teach that Good and Evil are not absolutes,' said Mother. Her voice strengthened. 'You teach that Right and Wrong are things to be negotiated or debated. You muddy the clear water of the Word of God. We do not need discussion. We need instruction. And you, Pastor ...' she pointed one bony finger at the minister '... you are

God's voice on Earth. Or should be. Yet I do not hear the Voice of God issuing from your mouth.' She turned now to the rest of the congregation. The silence was thick. Her voice rang out, clear and strong, gravid with conviction. 'I hear the voice of Satan, for it is Satan's job to cast doubt on that which does not harbour doubt, to confuse where there is clarity, to tempt us into believing we have rights to question the unquestionable. It is not the Lord's work that is being done in this church, Pastor. It is not the Lord's work at all.'

Pastor Bauer's smile could not withstand this onslaught. It withered. His colour rose. I watched his face as he struggled to control his temper.

'Surely you cannot accuse me of teaching evil, Mrs Cartwright. I preach only of tolerance and love. Do you seriously consider that to be the Devil's work?'

'Do you even believe in the Devil, Pastor?' Mother replied. 'Answer me that.'

I knew that Mother had played her trump card, even as I read the confusion in the pastor's face. His mouth opened and closed. Of course, later I understood the workings of his mind at that moment, the words he sought to explain his beliefs, the language he weighed and rejected. At the time, though, child that I was,

I knew there was only one possible response to Mother's question. The Devil was real. Of course he was real. To deny it was to deny the existence of God Himself. It was beyond contemplation.

'Mrs Cartwright ... I don't believe this is the forum for such discussion ... Perhaps ...'

'Answer the question, Pastor!' Mother shouted. I watched her mouth, saw the spittle fly in fine droplets. I knew hatred when I saw it. She exhaled it.

'I ... I believe that the Devil is a state of mind, Mrs Cartwright. An absence of God or a turning away from Him. The Devil is the evil within men.'

'Not real, then.' Mother's voice cracked with triumph.

'Of course, real,' said the pastor. 'Evil is very real. Unfortunately, we see the evidence all around us.'

'A real, physical presence, Pastor? An entity? A dark angel cast out from Heaven and residing in Hell? Or do you not believe in Hell either?'

Pastor Bauer swallowed. I could see irresolution in the workings of his expression. And then his face cleared.

'No,' he said. 'I do not believe in a physical Devil. I do not believe in a physical Hell. I believe these are metaphors to explain the nature of evil.'

I gasped. It is impossible to describe the betrayal I felt.

And in that moment, my mother was vindicated. She had exposed evil, and evil in the very place that should be a fortress against it. I saw her then transfigured – a saviour, a light burning in the darkness, a champion of Christ who had died for our sins. I loved her so intensely. I was consumed by it.

'You have heard!' screamed my mother. She had her back to the pastor now, addressing the congregation. 'You have heard from his own mouth. The Devil does not exist! Hell does not exist! Well, I know better. I read my Bible. And I believe it. I believe the Word of God!' She turned back towards the pulpit. 'I cannot remain in this nest of blasphemy,' she said. 'I seek the Light. I crave the Light. But I will pray for you, Mr Bauer. I will pray, even for you.'

We moved along the pew to the aisle. Mother's head was erect and she did not look back. I tried to imitate her strength, mirror her bearing. We walked proudly to the doors of the church and out into the morning sunshine. We strode in the direction of the farm. Mother looked back once, when we had travelled a few hundred metres. I did the same. The town was deserted, the doors of the church shut. Only later did I realise what she had been hoping to see. She wanted to witness an exodus, the congregation pouring from the place of evil in a tide towards the light and love of God.

But we were alone. Just us, the barren track and the pitiless sun.

'Whoa,' says Carly. 'So, that was, like, it, then? No more church?'

'No more church,' I say. 'No one else at all. From that point on, we worshipped at home. Even when we made our weekly trips to town, Mother didn't speak to anyone she didn't have to. She felt betrayed. She felt the sole guardian against the forces of evil. There was no one she could trust.'

'Apart from you.'

'Apart from me. And God.' I sigh and wipe my hand across my forehead. It is damp with sweat. 'You have no idea how heavy a burden that was.' I am suddenly assailed with tiredness, though it is still early. My sleep patterns have unravelled and lie in chaotic threads. 'So Mother got her wish. It was really her wish all along. Just the three of us — God, her and me — in our dusty garden of Eden. All evil banished.'

'You even had the apple trees,' says Carly.

'Yes,' I say. 'And the serpent, of course.'

'The serpent?'

'Adam. Adam was the serpent lurking under the tree all along. I just hadn't recognised him. But Mamma did. And when she discovered him, then whatever state of bliss we'd enjoyed was gone forever. I was cast out. To this day I am cast out.'

'How did she find him? What did she do?'

'Tomorrow,' I say. 'After your chicken and stuffing, I will tell you. This story is nearly done, Carly.' The ending is so close it dominates my vision. But there is something lurking behind it. I sense a presence, though I do not know what it is.

We sit for a few minutes more. The branches have freed the sun from their grasp and it is hot. The sky is clear and dusted with delicate blues. The lilies in the pond ride the water. Time goes on.

'Could you take me back inside, please, Carly?' I say. 'I am tired and a little hot.'

'Sure thing, Mrs C.'

She wheels me along the winding path, through sun-baked flower beds and wilting grass, to the French doors. Inside, the room is cool. The fan turns leisurely.

Someone has brightened my table with a vase of flowers, splashes of colour and life.

I feel content.

After Carly leaves, with many confirmations of time and arrangements for our dinner date, I doze awhile in my chair. There is a tingling in my arm, as if a fuse is slowly burning.

CHAPTER 17

JANE HELPS GET ME ready. She is excited for me. Excited that I am leaving, if only for a short time. I am excited also. It is possibly twenty years since I dined as a guest of someone else. Maybe longer. Is it absurd to feel excited about a roast dinner among strangers? It probably is, but I don't care.

'You have a fantastic time,' says Jane as she looks me up and down and brushes a stray strand of hair from my face. We had sorted through my clothing together. It had not taken long. When you reach my age, there is precious little point in a varied wardrobe. Every item was old-fashioned, dark and slightly damp. But at least the moths hadn't got into anything. We had chosen a long and shapeless dress with a spray of tired lace around the neckline. Something must have persuaded me to buy it many years ago, though why on earth I considered it desirable is lost in time. Jane shows me my reflection in the wardrobe mirror. I look like Whistler's mother a few years past her use-by date.

'I'm sure I will, dear.'

'No wild dancing when you get a few drinks in you either.'

'Spoilsport. I was hoping Carly and I would go along to a discotheque afterwards.'

Jane kisses me on the cheek.

'Bless you, Leah. No one has gone to a disco for at least twenty years.'

'Really? Why am I the last to find out these things?'

Carly bursts into the room at four forty-five. She brings the sunshine with her. Between the two, they lighten the gloom of my clothing. Behind Carly is a woman who is obviously her mother. I remember how I had envisaged her. Overweight and impossibly cheerful. I got half of it right. She is actually trim and impossibly cheerful. She beams at Jane and me and challenges us not to find the world a marvellous place. I don't have the energy to fight her.

'You must be Mrs Cartwright,' she says, striding

forward and extending her hand. 'I'm Jacky, Carly's mum.'

'I'm delighted to meet you,' I say, shaking her hand. It is cool and elegant. 'But please call me Leah.'

'Hi, Mrs C,' says Carly. 'You ready?'

'To rock and roll,' I reply. I wonder if her generation has heard of rock and roll. I wonder if Jacky's generation has heard of rock and roll.

'I'll get the wheelchair,' says Jane. 'Now just watch out for her, Jacky. Leah is a wild child.'

The car is huge, with chrome bars along the front and seats I have to climb up steps to reach. Jane helps me into the passenger seat and fastens my seat belt. I feel exhausted just sitting down. Then they fold the wheelchair and take it around the back. Carly hops into the back seat. In a few moments the car turns through the grounds and the Home swivels out of vision.

The journey takes about half an hour. Carly's mum chats to me.

'I understand you were a librarian before you retired, Leah.'

I wonder how she knows this. It is not something I have mentioned to her daughter.

'That's right,' I say. 'I was a librarian at a small country town not far from here for … oh, about forty years.'

'Carly told me you love books. I guess that must've been a perfect job for you.'

'It was. Until things changed. When I started, you didn't need any qualifications other than a love of reading and the energy to spread that love. I applied for the job when the library was built, got it on the grounds that I was known in the area and knew about books. I like to think I did a good job.'

'I'm sure you did. But you said things changed.'

I place my hand on the dashboard when we go round corners. I've never driven a car. Ultimately, I don't trust them.

'They did. As the library expanded, we took on new staff. For fifteen years I had worked there by myself. And the new staff had to have qualifications. They'd done courses and knew all manner of procedures. All I knew was the books themselves. If anyone asked for a particular book I could lead them exactly to where it sat on the shelves. I could tell you if it was out on loan and when it was due back. I could probably have told you who had borrowed it. All that information was stored in my head. Then there was the Dewey Decimal system and file cards. Now there are computers and shelves of untouched books. What does a library become when books are no longer central? In many ways I'm glad I worked when I did, got out of it when I did.'

Jacky laughs.

'I wish *I* could get out of teaching,' she says. 'Too much bureaucracy, too many meetings. It's like the kids are an afterthought. I'm too old. At least, that's what Carly tells me. Isn't that right, sweetheart?'

There is no reply. She glances over her shoulder.

'In her own world,' she says to me. 'Gets her iPod plugged into her ears and nothing else exists. It's infuriating.'

'You must be very proud of your children,' I say. 'Carly is a delight, and her brother, doing medicine at university.'

She glances at me.

'Sorry?'

'Your son. Carly's brother.'

'I think you must be mistaken,' she says. There is an edge to her voice. 'Carly *had* a brother, but he died ten years ago. Leukaemia.'

It hurts, but I crane my neck to peer into the back seat. Fine white wires trail from Carly's ears. Her head moves to an imperceptible beat. She smiles and rewards me with a small wave. I smile back and hope it's more realistic than it feels.

'I'm so sorry, dear,' I say to Jacky. 'I am old and my memory plays tricks. I obviously have my stories confused.'

I gaze out of the window. The child had a story. And I missed it. I missed it completely. It is true that I am old and confused. But I am not so old and confused that I cannot be awed by the complexities and wonders of the human mind.

Jacky guides the car into the driveway of a large house. It has a garden with neat borders and there are white pillars bookmarking the front door. She cuts the engine and Carly slides out. I stay in the car until they have assembled my wheelchair and helped me into it. The front door opens and a man steps outside. He is smiling. Cheerfulness appears to be in Carly's genetic make-up.

'Mrs Cartwright,' he says. 'Welcome.'

He is not overweight either. And he's not wearing a suit. It is annoying when reality refuses to match my fiction.

'Thank you,' I reply. 'It's lovely to be here.'

* * *

I survive dinner.

The food is very good, but my appetite withered years ago. They serve me an impossibly large portion which only diminishes my hunger further. I feel guilty. When I have eaten all I can, what remains on my plate appears larger than the portion I started with. I wonder if I will be able to make it through the evening without visiting the bathroom. The practicalities are daunting. The possibilities of disaster more so.

Conversation is bright and cheerful. It couldn't fail to be.

Once I have turned down dessert, Carly's parents clear the table.

'Carly told us you would be finishing your story tonight, Leah,' says her mother. 'So, if you don't mind, we'll leave you to it. If there's anything you need, just let Carly know, okay?'

'Thank you so much. You are very kind.'

'Would you care for a drink? A sherry perhaps?'

'A glass of water would be fine,' I say. 'Alcohol and I were never the best of friends. I severed our relationship a long time ago.'

'Of course.'

The dining room is pleasant. The furniture is expensive and in good taste. It reminds me of what used to be called an 'entertaining room'. There are two armchairs in front of an ornate fireplace, unlit in the balmy evening air. Carly helps me from my dining chair to an armchair. I sink into its depths and know that without help I would never achieve the vertical again. Carly takes the chair opposite.

'Recording machine?' I say.

'Got it, Mrs C,' she says. 'But before you start, I just want to say something. You know, about all that stuff. When we sort of fell out. My story? Yeah? You were interested in how I met Josh. My boyfriend? And I kind of blew you off.'

'You don't have to tell me anything, my dear.'

'Yeah, yeah. I know. But there is something I wanted to discuss with you. And it's not something I can really talk about to my folks, you know. It's not a story. Not like you tell. But ... I dunno. I just wanted to talk about it.'

'Is it sexual?'

'What?' Her face creases. 'No. Nothing about sex. Jeez, Mrs C. But I guess I want your advice. About love.'

'Ah. Love is something I know a little about.'

'Well.' She folds her legs beneath her. It is an effort-less movement. I wonder how many years it has been since I was able to do that. I wonder if I have *ever* been able to do that. 'You know how I said I saw Josh when he was playing his guitar. And how he was really into it. Into the playing. And that's what attracted me to him. Well...' She reaches to twist her eyebrow stud. 'It's just that Josh is really, really good at music. He plays in this band and they're popular. There's even been talk of a contract. With a music company, you know? And...'

'Yes?' I say.

'Now he's sorta bigger than he was. Do you see what I mean?'

'No.'

'He's like more than Josh. More than the dorky kid I saw who was into music. And he's popular. With every-one. He's become uber-cool.'

Uber-cool?

'And you are worried your feelings are changing?' I reply.

'No. I mean, yes. They *are* changing. I'm so into him. More than ever. It's just there are pressures.'

'Ah!' I begin to see the problem. 'Is he pressuring you into sex before you are ready?'

'Jeez, no.' Carly plucks at her lower lip and smiles. I am rewarded with a glimpse of ornamental dental work. 'What is it with you, Mrs C? You're, like, obsessed with sex. There *are* other things, you know.'

'Well, perhaps you could be more forthright, Carly. I can't advise you unless I understand the nature of the problem.'

'It's… Look, am I good enough? That's what I want to know. Am I good enough for him?'

There is a slight pain in my chest. Indigestion. That's the problem with the substitution of decent food for inedible steak and black-eyed potatoes. It has taken my digestive system by surprise. A culinary ambush.

'Are you good enough for this Josh of yours? Is that what you are asking?'

Carly nods.

I shift my weight in the chair. It eases the burning slightly.

'Listen,' I say. 'I don't know this young man of yours, but I think I have learned something about you. And I will tell you what I see. You are a beautiful girl. You have exceptionally fine bone structure. But that's not important. That kind of beauty might be the kind in vogue right now so you are fortunate, I suppose, to possess it.

But what has nothing to do with chance is your inner beauty. It shines through you and brightens wherever you are. You have an enormous capacity for love, Carly. I feel it, like warmth from a fire.'

She cups her face in her hands and stares at me. I detect a reddening of her cheeks.

'Aw, Mrs C...'

'I have not finished. You are extraordinary. Do not ask if you are good enough for him. Consider whether he is good enough for you. He should be grateful to be in a position to earn your love. And if he is not, if he ever looks at you like you are something less than the greatest prize he could ever win, then ... then ...'

'What?'

'Tell him to piss off.'

There is silence for a heartbeat. And then Carly laughs. She laughs so hard that tears run down her cheeks. I rummage in my bag, produce a dog-eared photograph.

'Here is his photograph,' I say. 'I don't need it anymore.'

'Mrs C...'

'I don't *want* it anymore. I will swap it for one of you, if you have a spare and you don't mind a sentimental old woman having it. But you can keep this.'

She takes it.

'Jeez, Mrs C. I wasn't saying he was *bad*, or anything. This is about me, not him.'

'It is *only* about you, Carly. It is about the love you deserve. And now I want you to listen one more time. Because my story is coming to an end. And it is a story about just this very thing. Do you want to know why I never married? Why I never had a boyfriend, after Adam? Because after his love, I knew there was no point in settling for anything less. I *couldn't* settle for anything less.'

'He'd do anything for you, huh?'

'He sacrificed himself for me,' I say. My words sound small even to my own ears. 'He loved me so much he sacrificed himself. Would your young man do that for you?'

I find my own face is moist. I brush tears away with a wrinkled hand. It seems somehow apart from me.

'Turn on that machine,' I say.

She does.

CHAPTER 18

For a while, we established the old routine on the farm.

Mother wrote every morning while I spent my time with Adam. I no longer entirely trusted the orchards. They weren't as safe as they had been. Yet they provided the protection of cover and were swollen, ripe, with memories and emotions. I didn't allow Adam anywhere near the house. And yet he still left evidence. I saw it everywhere and spent hours removing it. It pained Adam that he couldn't be with me. It carved changes in his face. He grew thinner, gaunt. And his spirit seemed to shrivel. When I left him to return home, he would watch me until I disappeared. He never moved a muscle, just stood there as if the sole reason for his existence was disappearing forever.

At night I watched the moon through my window. It scuttled through clouds and spilled light on my face. But my chair — the twin of the one in Mother's room where Adam had appeared that first night, swinging his legs into and out of shadow — remained empty. The foot of my bed gathered nothing now but dust. I curled into myself, hugged my memories and rode the pain to troubled sleep.

The only time I relaxed was during the hours Mother was writing. At all other times we would be together. Or if not, I knew she might appear at any moment. She had not forgotten the intruder. Sometimes she would make us search together. She nestled the shotgun in her arms, cradled it like a baby, and we swept the area around the house, widening the circle until we reached the furthest boundaries of the orchard. She never found anything, but that didn't stop her searching.

From nine until midday, however, I was safe. I took my book out onto the verandah, stayed there for ten minutes. Glancing through the kitchen window, I checked that Mother's angular frame remained bent over her task, her hand moving regularly, the ink filling up white space.

Then I descended the steps, missing the third which always creaked. I padded softly away. Then ran. Ran so the wind made my hair dance. Ran so my dress pressed against my flying legs and moulded to my muscles. Ran to the orchard.

To Adam.

To Adam who waited for me, perched on the branch of an apple tree or sitting cross-legged on the ground, splitting blades of grass. When I appeared at the mouth of the avenue, his face cleared. His pinched expression, the stormy emotions that darkened his skin, were blown away by the squall of my arrival. He stood and I rushed into his arms. I felt his hair against my cheek and smelled the maleness of him. The scent of sweat and sun and summer rain. And occasionally, something else. Looking back, I think it was the smell of mortality.

One day. The last day. A Wednesday.

I was fifteen years old.

I lay on my back, my head resting on Adam's stomach. He stroked my cheek. I watched the boughs of the apple tree, the canopy above. Leaves stirred listlessly in the heavy air. As they parted I caught glimpses of the sky beyond, tantalising peeks of the infinite before the veils of green closed once more. I checked my internal clock.

I had another hour before I would have to return to the house and help Mother prepare lunch.

'Adam?' I said.

He grunted. There was drowsiness in the noise, as if I'd caught him in that moment when sleep had breached the wall of wakefulness and was on the verge of victory.

'Why do you love me?' I asked.

'What?'

'Why do you love me?'

His fingers stopped their stroking. His leg, crooked before, straightened. The muscles in his stomach tensed.

'I don't know.'

'That,' I said, 'is not the right answer. Please. You must be able to tell me.' There was a protracted silence, long enough to breed within me a worm of wriggling doubt. It grew as quickly as it was born, developed teeth and chewed to the surface. I rolled onto my side and gazed into his face. 'You *do* love me, don't you?'

'Yes,' he said. And it was the most simple of affirmatives. As if I had asked a question that required no contemplation. It simply *was*.

'Why?'

He closed his eyes. Long lashes curled against olive skin. Then he opened them again. I felt there was a danger of falling into their depths, spinning down forever. And I knew I would not regret the descent for one moment. I would revel in it.

'I can't explain, Leah. All I know is that there is nothing more … precious in this world than you. Ask me anything and I will do it. Without doubt, without regret.' He smiled and brushed my cheek. 'I've told you before. *You* are the expert with words. Don't ask me to explain.'

It was all I wanted, all I needed. I closed my eyes and lay my head against his arm. The air was heavy with the scent of apples and the drone of insects.

'Leah?'

The word hit me with the violence of a fist, though it was quietly spoken. I was on my feet in one movement. Blood pulsed in my brain. I was dimly aware of Adam standing next to me.

But all my attention was taken by the figure of Mother halfway down the avenue of apple trees. She looked at me and then at Adam. What I saw in her gaze made me feel my heart was being torn in two. There was incomprehension. And then a flood of betrayal. She withered, grew old before my eyes.

Mother turned on her heels and strode in the direction of the house, her long black dress flapping.

'Mamma!' I screamed.

And then I ran after her, my heart, lungs and legs pumping.

I intercepted Mother a hundred metres from the house. In the periphery of my vision I caught a glimpse of Adam emerging from the avenue of apple trees. I put the image out of mind.

'Mamma,' I said, stepping in front of her. She kept walking, her face a stone, and I was forced to scamper backwards. 'Mamma, please. I can explain.'

She stopped then. She looked at me as if I were a stranger.

'Can you, Leah? Then explain.'

I didn't see the blow coming. My head snapped to the side. A fraction of a second later I heard the crack of flesh on flesh. The burning of my cheek followed slowly. I didn't raise a hand to my face. I straightened and looked directly into her eyes.

'It is not what you think,' I said. My voice did not quaver and I was grateful. I didn't know why it was important, but I felt it.

'You are a whore! A jezebel!' For the first time, Mother's voice was raised, her face contorted. I felt the pain pulsing from her. It stung worse than her blow.

'No, Mamma. I am not. I am not.'

The second slap came from the other side. This time I saw it coming, but did nothing to avoid it. I knew I deserved punishment, that my pain was a rightful price to pay. I also knew this pain was nothing compared to the spiritual suffering I must undergo later, my knees on the hard wood of the verandah, the words of contrition that would wring my soul until it was dry.

Even so. Even so. I thought I understood what I did. But it turned out I knew nothing about the real nature of pain. I was merely on the brink of knowledge.

'You are a liar and a whore!' screamed Mother. 'You have lain with that boy. I saw you. Dear God, I wish my eyes had been torn from their sockets before they had ever witnessed such a sight. My daughter. A whore.'

'Mamma,' I said. 'I will tell you the truth. I swore to you that I would always tell you the truth. Listen. I beg you. Listen to me. Please, Mamma.'

I sank to my knees.

I kept my eyes fixed on Mother's boots as I babbled. How Adam had appeared at Daddy's funeral. A small boy. My imaginary friend who grew as my imagination grew, whose spirit took on bodily form over the years, became … himself. I tried to explain why I thought I had made him. To combat the void left when my father placed a gun barrel into his mouth and pulled a trigger? To fill the gap that might have been filled with children my own age, at school perhaps?

I told her everything. I left out nothing. And with each word, I felt cleansed. For I had always felt that I had been less than honest with Mother, that I had withheld. I had not lied. But I had withheld. And she deserved better. She was my mother and I loved her.

When I was done, all words spent, I kept my head lowered. The silence was sharp, but I didn't know if forgiveness or anger honed it. I looked up.

Mamma had a fist to her mouth. Her eyes were wild. There were tears on her face. I could not remember the last time I had seen her cry. I felt a surge of hope.

'My God,' she whispered. 'My God, what have you done?'

I reached out towards her leg.

'I don't know, Mamma,' I said. 'What have I done?'

Her scream made my blood run cold. It was something primitive, primeval. If I had not seen her mouth twisted in agony I wouldn't have believed her capable of uttering it. Her hand raked across my cheek. But this time it was not the flat of her palm. It was nails that tore at my flesh. I lifted a hand to my face and it came away red. And then her fingers were entangled in my hair. Mamma yanked me to my feet. I felt my scalp stretch and tear. She had both hands in my hair now, pulling and ripping. The pain made my eyes fill. It occupied all my being, so that her words came as if from a distance.

'Do you not see?' she screamed. 'Do you not see what you have done? You have brought evil here, Leah. Into our world. You have been corrupted by the Devil and that ... that creature is his spawn. Here to tempt you into wickedness. How could you create something like that? It is only God who can create. Or the Devil to taint His purity. And the Devil has used your vanity to pursue his own ends. To harness the evil that lies within you.'

'No, Mamma. Adam is not evil. I am not.'

'You lie. You are so full of sin, you cannot taste your lies. But they are foul, girl. Your very breath reeks of corruption.'

The blows came faster now. Mother put all her strength into them. My lip burst and lights exploded in my head. I tried to cover my skull with my hands, but she found a way through. The thought blossomed through pain. She means to kill me. My mother means to kill me.

When the pressure eased and then fell away, I thought for a moment that she had re-considered. I opened an eye that was already starting to swell and close. And what I saw did not, at first, make sense. I shook my head to clear illusions.

Adam had his fingers around mother's throat. Her face was distorted in pain and fear. Already I could see her skin changing colour, suffused with purple as oxygen fled. She flayed at his arms, but her strength had gone. Terror lived behind her eyes.

And Adam? Adam was expressionless. The muscles in his arms bunched as he increased the pressure. Sweat stood on his forehead. And the worst part was the silence. The sky and earth looked on and were silent.

'Adam, no!' I screamed, but he didn't appear to hear me. His eyes bored into my mother's. I tried to tear his hands away, but he was too strong. I brought my face as close to his as I could.

'Adam,' I said. 'If you love me, you will let her go. Please, Adam? Let her go. For the love you bear me.'

For a moment, nothing happened. Then his eyes focused once more. He saw me. And his hands dropped.

Mother fell to the ground, gasping. I threw myself beside her and cradled her head in my hands. She coughed and her eyes bulged. But as her lungs tore at the air, her skin lightened, became tinged with pink. I cried. And they were tears of relief.

It took a few minutes before she was able to speak. Her words were little more than croaks, but they pierced me to the heart.

'Do you deny the Devil's evil, Leah? Do you deny it still?'

I looked up and met Adam's eyes. He occupied them once more. But all I read within his gaze was defeat. I knew then … then … thomething … happening … thomething …

'Mrs C?' Carly sits up in her chair. Her eyes flash with alarm. 'Are you all right?'

There is a numbness on the left side of my face. My mouth sags and a thin trail of drool leaks. I need to answer her. I am not all right. My brain sends orders to my mouth, but the message doesn't arrive. It is strange. I see the words ordered beautifully in my mind. I know which to select. But my body is an idiot.

'Thomething…' I say. 'Thomething…'

After that there is bustle and lights and movement. But most of it passes me by.

THE BEGINNING

And was all the time merging with a unique endeavour
To bring to bloom the million-petalled flower
Of being here.
Next time you can't pretend there'll be anything else …

CHAPTER 19

I AM THE CENTRE.

Everything else is vague. There is a harsh light somewhere. I am lying in a sea of white. My body feels dry and shrivelled and weightless. A husk. The smallest breeze will sweep me away, tumble me towards a void. I close my eyes to seek it. Find it.

'Mrs Cartwright?'

The voice is a summons I don't want to obey, but it is insistent. The only way to make it go away is to acknowledge it. I do not know how I know this. I just know. I open my eyes.

The light is still there. A face swims before it. I do

not recognise the face, but I am not sure that means anything. The light paints a nimbus around it. An angel with pockmarked skin and a thin moustache.

'Can you hear me, Mrs Cartwright?' says the mundane angel.

I attempt to send a message from the centre, but the practicalities are beyond me. I blink my eyes instead.

'You are in hospital, Mrs Cartwright,' he says. 'You have had a stroke, but you are stable now. Do not try to talk. What you need, more than anything, is rest.'

I was resting. Why summon me to tell me to rest? I don't understand.

She has red hair and a face I know. She holds my hand.

There are machines around me. From the corners of my eyes I see lights blinking and lines that run, fade, renew themselves. Tubes grow from the withered flesh of my arm. It is my flesh, but outside of me. I am the centre. Little else is real.

'Oh, Leah,' says the woman with red hair. She is weeping and she holds my hand too hard. I know her. I think I loved her in another place and another time. She brushes her eyes with a hand and tries for a smile. Her aim is off. It comes out twisted.

'You're looking *much* better, sweetie. We were worried about you there, for a while. But if there's one thing I've learned about Leah Cartwright it's that she's a tough old bird. Keeps coming back for more. You'll be on your feet before you know it, so you will.' She is gathering momentum. I feel her words are masking something, that maybe she spills them to avoid thinking. I don't know. 'Everyone from home sends their love and warmest wishes for a speedy recovery. I have a card.' She holds it up before my face. It is full of writing, but I cannot make any of it out. 'I'll put it on your bedside. And then there are the flowers. Have you seen the flowers? They are beautiful. A massive bouquet. Can you smell them? It's like summer in this room, Leah.'

Her name is Jane. I want to taste the word in my mouth, but I can't.

I find strength from somewhere, channel it into what remains of nerves and sinew and muscle. I squeeze her hand and watch her eyes widen, fill with wonder.

'The baby, Leah,' she says and her voice is drenched in the exultation of mystery. 'It moved. My baby moved. She kicked.'

She laughs, a hymn to life. My mouth twitches.

Everything is quickening. It is as it should be.

She continues talking, a torrent of language. I like the drone of words. They mingle with the hisses of the machines, become a lullaby that rocks me to sleep.

Time passes and I occupy a little more of myself. Now I feel myself as a centre that pushes outwards, nearly to the limit of a wasted body. I cannot control it. No, I cannot do that. But I am me. I am Leah Cartwright. My mind is battered, but working. Memories are more vivid than the room I know I will not leave. I can move parts of my body, though it takes an extraordinary effort of will. I even manage to speak one or two words, but they are poor and mangled things. I smile and it is lopsided. The muscles on the left side of my face refuse to cooperate. The building is crumbling, but I am a tenant yet.

Carly and her parents visit me. They come camouflaged behind a mass of blooms. Birnam wood has come to Dunsinane. A nurse relieves them of their burden and they sit by my bed. An awkward silence follows. I cannot break it.

'We are so sorry, Mrs Cartwright,' says Carly's mother finally. I cannot remember her name. She smiles, but her eyes are filmed with tears. The room's lights are reflected in them. She takes my hand. Everyone wants to take my hand. Perhaps it reassures them I am still here. 'We feel ... responsible for what happened. For a few dreadful moments we thought it was the food. You know. That we had poisoned you. Botulism, or something. And then the paramedics said they thought it might have been a stroke and we, well we got to thinking that maybe it had all been too much for you, that we had brought this on somehow and we just felt dreadful about it, I can't tell you how dreadful we felt, still feel, but so relieved you seem to be on the mend ...'

A dam has been breached and the guilt pours out. I want to tell her that I am the one who should feel responsible, that I nearly brought tragedy into their ordered lives, infected their home with the disease of death. But words are no longer my slaves. I smile and hope she listens to that.

Carly hovers in the background. I am impatient to see her, but must receive her parents' apology first. It takes an eternity. The father feels he must give an encore to his wife's performance. Finally, they bring the curtain down. Her mother bends and kisses me on the cheek.

'We'll leave you with Carly for a few moments, Mrs Cartwright. The nurse said we shouldn't stay long, that you need rest. But we'll be back to see you very soon.'

They leave as if having shed a burden other than the weight of flowers.

Carly sits on a chair beside my bed There is something different about her and it is not just the concern she wears. Or the make-up, which has made a reappearance. She attempts a smile and that is when I see it. Her teeth. Strong, white, even and free.

'Hey, Mrs C,' she says. 'Had the braces off yesterday. Whatya reckon?' I think she must have read the direction of my gaze and the widening of my eyes. She parts her lips, offers an uninterrupted view. I want to tell her I am pleased for her and saddened for myself. That I miss her iridescent smile. I nod instead.

She edges her chair closer.

'Got to tell you something. Josh has a gig tonight. It's major. Support band for a big name playing at this club in the city and he's hyper about it. So last night, he goes, "Do you want to come with us in the van with the band?" and I tell him I can't make it, that I'm coming in to see you. And he's, like, "What?" Doesn't compute with him, that I'd sooner visit you than be a hanger-on in a club. So I say there'll be other times.'

I would feel guilty, but it's obvious she's building to something.

'So he says maybe I should get my priorities right, that there'll be other times when I could visit *you*. Then he comes out with something really shitty, but I can't remember exactly the words he used. It was more what he nearly said, you know what I mean? Anyway, he hints there are other chicks who'd be only too happy to come with the band, only he doesn't quite say it like that. So I say to him, "Would you do anything for me, Josh? Like without thinking about it?" and he goes "What are you on about?" as if it's the dumbest thing anyone has ever asked. So I say ...' She laughs and it is pure and white. 'I say, "Piss off, Josh." Just like that. Out of the blue. You should have seen his face. It was like I'd smacked him.'

I look for sadness and regret in *her* face, but detect no signs.

'And you know what, Mrs C? I'm glad I said it. Things had ... I don't know. Got unbalanced, I guess. You made me see that. I was way too grateful for any attention he gave and that meant he had all the power. I mean *I'd* given him the power. And he was prepared to use it. Not only that, he was enjoying using it. So ... well, maybe we'll make up and maybe we won't. But if we do make up then it'll be on my terms as well, not just his. And if we don't, then that's okay, too. Seriously. I reckon I'm developing a mind of my own. Are you proud of me, Mrs C?'

I am. I wish I could tell her. I try to write it on my face.

A nurse enters and tells Carly to leave. I cannot let her go. Not yet. So I grab her hand. Just that small movement drains me. I summon all my reserves of will, channel it into my mouth. My tongue is a slab of meat and my lips are dead. I force them to a semblance of life.

'Story,' I say. The word comes out maimed and my voice is cracked and dry. I summon a little extra energy. 'Machine. Carly.'

Her face clouds.

'Hey, Mrs C. There's time to finish your story. When you get some strength back, okay?'

'No.' This time, my voice is firm. It needs to be. Time is drifting, slipping away. 'Tomorrow. Story.'

'Jeez, Mrs C...'

'Tomorrow.'

She reads my face for a minute or so. I do not know what script she deciphers, but it must be enough. She nods.

'Sure. Tomorrow. I'll be here. And I'll bring my machine. Okay? Satisfied?'

I close my eyes.

'Oh, I nearly forgot. I brought you a present.'

I open my eyes again.

'It's a lousy photograph. I look like a total dork. Anyway, we bought a frame and everything, on our way in. I mean, you *did* ask, Mrs C. God knows why you want it. But here you are.'

I bring the frame close to my face. My right hand trembles under its weight.

Carly smiles at me from within the photograph. Her teeth are enclosed in a rainbow. The frame is thinly plated silver and has small hearts embossed at regular intervals around the perimeter. I close my eyes and hug it to my chest.

CHAPTER 20

THE RED LIGHT BLINKS.

Carly brings the machine close to my face. My voice is little more than a whisper. But inside my head, the words march bright, clear and confident. They follow my orders. They line up in perfect ranks. Not one rebels.

I examine the images behind my eyes. I see it all from the outside. The woman in the dark dress is crumpled on the earth, one hand to her neck. A purple bruise is flowering there. The girl is on her knees in the dust. She has hair the colour of midnight. It catches the sun. Her face is fresh and unlined, though if one looks carefully there is knowledge amongst the innocence. And one can trace the journey of that face through time to come. As the years unroll, the knowledge will spread, a canker on the bloom, until innocence has fled forever. Becomes a memory only. But now … now the bruise is in its first flush. Now she is between two worlds, clinging to each as they slide inexorably apart. The boy stands, his eyes downcast. His hair is a mass of dark curls. There is tension in his limbs as if he is on a hair-trigger of flight.

The world is inside my head. Past and present and future are rolled together. Everything is inside my head.

The woman speaks.

'You cannot have both, Leah. You cannot embrace God with one arm and the Devil with the other. You cannot be with me and … consort with abominations. Choose, Leah. Choose between the light and the dark. Choose one and cast out the other. For the love of God and the love of me.'

The boy turns his eyes towards the mother and daughter, regards them for a moment. Then he takes a step forward. The woman recoils, slithers away a metre in a puff of dust, clutches at the crucifix around her neck. The girl raises her face. He bends and traces with a finger the snail track of tears on her cheeks, puts the finger to his lips and tastes the saltiness there. He turns and walks away. Towards the looming apple trees in the distance. He doesn't look back.

The girl scrambles to her feet and runs after him, stops, turns. The bonds that tie her spirit tear and split. Agony is written on her body.

'Choose, Leah,' her mother croaks.

The boy shrinks and disappears in shadow. The trees swallow him. The girl holds out a hand to her mother, helps her to her feet. They stand for a moment, fingers entwined. Then the girl drops her head and her hand, turns and walks away. She moves slowly, follows the boy into darkness.

The air is cool and sweet beneath the trees. It smells of fruit. Apples lie on the ground and some are bruised, discoloured. Beneath the scent of growing things there is the tinge of corruption and decay. She walks on, dappled in light and shadow.

The boy sits halfway down the avenue. He splits a blade of grass between his nails and doesn't look up as she approaches. The girl sits beside him, plucks a blade herself. They work at green flesh in silence.

'I love you, Adam,' she says finally.

He keeps his head bent over his work.

'I know,' he says.

'And I love my mother.'

'I know.'

She throws the shredded blade away and buries her face in her hands. Sobs rack her. The boy puts an arm around her shoulders and draws her to him. She folds into the crook between his chin and shoulder. He feels the cold drip of tears. Then he lowers her to the ground so they are lying face to face. He kisses her gently, feathers her cheeks and lips. She puts a hand behind his head and draws him closer, kisses him harder. She feels his body against hers, presses herself into his flesh as if she would be absorbed by him. She loves for the last time.

The sun dips further in the sky, peeks below the level of trees. Her skin tingles with its caress. She reaches out and brushes the boy's hair away from his eyes.

'I cannot choose,' she says. Her voice is not wet with emotion, but bruised with despair. 'I cannot.'

He sits up and takes her hand in his.

'I understand,' he says. 'Which is why I must. Come with me, Leah.'

They stand, walk further along the avenue. He keeps her hand in his. Shadows change the landscape. Darkness sprouts from the ground and trees thicken and crowd. The path they tread narrows, forces them together. Branches droop, the leaves and their shadows merge. Dark walls rise.

The boy stops. The girl glances over her shoulder. She can no longer see the pathway through trees. There is no sound, except their own breathing. Their breaths mist against the darkness. The air is tingly with cold.

'Here,' says the boy, reaching forward and parting the darkness. He steps through. The girl follows. Leaves caress her as they part. She moves into light.

They stand on the summit of a mountain. A dizzying drop yawns beneath. On all sides, ice and snow glitters. The girl glances at her feet, a step from the brink. She shuffles backwards. The sky is powdered blue, dusted with wisps of cloud. The sun is swollen gold. Mountains crowd on all sides, but her eyes are drawn from them. Down, down, down into a patch of green in the valley below.

A winding road, as delicate as a pencil line on green paper, leads to a castle, its walls buttery in light. A thin ribbon of moat sparkles. The turrets, four, five, six, point towards Heaven. Each is capped with red. From this height she can see no movement, but the girl screws her eyes and sees thin windows stencilled on the walls. She knows people move there and they are happy.

'It's as beautiful as I remember,' she says.

It is a page from a book. It is a page from a distant childhood.

The boy lets go of her hand and steps towards the edge. She moves to stop him, but her limbs won't obey. He turns to face her, his back to the brink. He puts a finger to his lips.

'Everything you can imagine is real,' he says. 'Remember that, Leah. And know, too, that I will always be with you. Inside your head. Nothing, no one, can take that away.'

She wants to scream, but cannot. She wants to move, but cannot.

The boy spreads his arms wide, raises his face to the heavens. His face glows with the kiss of the sun. Then he topples slowly backwards. Time stutters. Stops, moves again. For a brief moment their eyes lock. And he is gone.

She finds her body again, rushes to the edge, drops to her knees. Far below, the boy's body floats and shrinks in air. He turns leisurely as he drops, becomes smaller and smaller, a dark smudge against the green fields with their pencilled roads. He becomes a speck.

He becomes nothing.

A scream tears at her throat, but doesn't come out.

The valley below is washed in shade. The castle swims and fades, eaten by the dark. It is as if a page has turned, the final page of a story and the endpaper is black. The mist of her breath dissolves and dies. She is on her knees in the orchard. One world has returned and another has gone forever. She knows it has gone forever. An apple lies on the ground. Something has burrowed beneath its flesh. Its perfection is blemished by a dark bruise that she knows will spread and spread until all that was green and good is consumed by darkness and time.

The girl staggers to her feet. The world is muted, the birds do not sing. She turns towards home, towards her mother and towards her future. Nothing, she knows, will ever be the same.

'Let. Me. Listen.'

The words sound faint to my ears. I wonder if anything I have said has been picked up by her machine. I need to know if the story is out there, beyond my head. I need to know.

Carly has an expression on her face I have difficulty reading. It might be pity. It might be horror. Her hand trembles as she presses buttons on her machine. Then a stranger's voice scratches at the air. It is a thin voice and it chips at words, extracts them one by one. Barely a minute elapses before the sound subsides into nothingness.

I have spoken no more than four or five sentences. But they are enough. For me, if not for Carly. If I had the energy, I would lament the disparity between what is in my head and the poor, withered version that whispers at my ear. It is cruel evidence that everything has been stripped from me. Words were the last, and the most precious, gift to desert me.

Most precious, save one.

But it is enough.

I close my eyes. I am so tired. I barely feel the brush of Carly's lips against my cheek, barely hear her promise to see me again tomorrow.

I sleep with guilt. I wanted to say goodbye to the child. The girl with a boy living in her head.

But perhaps it is better this way.

CHAPTER 21

IT IS A TROUBLED NIGHT. Images, memories and dreams crowd me.

I wait for something, but I do not know what it is. I am no longer afraid. I am … curious.

The blinds in my room are closed against the dawn. It lends the air a sinister aspect, as if time has frozen. Or as if I have frozen and somewhere the world goes on without me. Even the sounds from outside are muted.

The doctor with the pockmarked face and thin moustache bursts in. It jolts me from an almost permanent doze. He is followed by a group of people in white coats. They assemble around the end of my bed. I cannot make out individual faces, but they appear impossibly young. Can they be medically trained? It seems absurd. But then everyone is young nowadays.

The doctor pats my hand and utters meaningless greetings. His smile is practised. Then he peers into my eyes and takes my pulse. I suspect we both wonder if there is a point to this. He turns to the group. They gaze back, a row of pale faces suspended above clipboards. One or two shuffle from foot to foot.

'This patient,' says the doctor, 'has suffered a stroke. There are two types of stroke. They are?'

Nearly everyone raises a hand. The question, apparently, is easy.

'Yes, Dr Patton.'

'Ischaemic and haemorrhagic, sir.'

'Correct. And the difference?'

He chooses someone else.

'Sir. An ischaemic stroke develops when a blood clot blocks a blood vessel in the brain. A haemorrhagic stroke develops when an artery in the brain leaks or bursts, causing bleeding inside the brain or near the surface of the brain.'

'Very good.'

I'm not sure it is very good, but I cannot say anything.

'And how can we tell the difference between them? Yes, Dr Singh.'

'A CT scan, possibly followed by an MRI, sir.'

'Excellent. Mrs ...' He examines his own clipboard. '... Cartwright has suffered an ischemic stroke, the lesser of two evils. What treatment would be appropriate once her condition is diagnosed?'

This group is knowledgeable. Once again, nearly all hands are raised. But one figure detaches from the others, moves to the blinds. No one pays attention. I see him dimly, across the room.

'A tissue plasminogen activator, sir. Common aspirin can also be used with a t-PA. Or aspirin combined with some other antiplatelet medication.'

'Aspirin and t-PA together, doctor?'

There is something in his tone that strikes caution in the group. It's as if they are wary of being tripped up. No one replies.

'The use of aspirin within twenty-four hours of t-PA can be very dangerous for a patient,' says the pock-marked doctor. There is triumph in his voice. He has produced a trump card. The group of white coats sags a little. 'Anyway, time passes. Let's move on.'

He leaves my room without acknowledging me. The

group files past my bed. A few of them smile. I would smile back, but one side of my mouth droops uselessly. The door closes. Somewhere a clock ticks.

I let the absence of voices wash over me. It is a luxurious bath. Nothing out there is as vivid as the contents of my mind. I retreat into it.

The images are jumbled. They flood over me in a waterfall. My mother's death when I was thirty-nine, still living at home, the orchards wilted and baking and dying in the sun. I found her kneeling at the side of her bed. Her face was radiant with joy, as if the man on the cross had stepped down and personally ushered her into light. I cried for three days, wandering through an empty house. Pastor Bauer, grey now and lined, argued to the town council that I would make a perfect librarian. The library itself, surrounded by books, endless days of inhaling the dust of covers, inhaling stories. The journeys I took between countless pages, though never again did I journey as I did with Adam. Millions of words. Millions of beautiful words. Friends gained and friends lost. A plan, hatched one summer with a new woman at the library, to visit Italy and England. I so desperately wanted to get back to the London in my head. It never happened, though the reason is gone forever. I try, but I cannot remember. And men. Yes, one or two men showed interest in me. One even proposed. And I thought — I remember thinking — should I accept? Is it better to accept second best than spend a lifetime alone?

I never regretted turning him down. And that realisation answers my question.

So many thoughts. So many memories.

And now it has all come to this.

The shadows gather in the room. There is a movement to my right. It might be a breeze finding its way through the slats of the blind. I turn my head. This takes time and energy.

There is a cabinet against the wall and next to it a chair. Narrow bands of sunlight leak through the blind and coat everything in stripes. Something else. On the chair. A pair of legs. They do not swing because they touch the floor. But ... maybe it is the way the light filters. Maybe it gives the illusion of movement, of small legs swinging, swinging. Above the legs, a figure lost in shadows. I remember the group. I remember how one member detached himself. My heart flutters in my chest. It feels frail, a caged bird weakening with every struggling beat of its wings against bars.

'Hello?' I say. 'Who's there?'

My voice rings clear and true. There is no crack or tremor. There is no age. The sound is sharp with youth.

And that's when I know.

'Adam,' I say.

The legs stop their movement, the dark shape rises from the chair. He turns the bar that hangs beside the blind and sunlight floods the room. I smell apples. He moves towards my bed, sits on the edge, takes my hand.

'Adam,' I say.

His hair is snow white, though it still curls. His face is a nest of wrinkles, jowls loose and drooping, skin parchment dry. But his eyes. His eyes are the same. Liquid with life and love. He smiles and squeezes my hand.

'Hello, Leah.'

'You've come back to me.'

I am ashamed of my words even as they leave my lips. They mock me. I have waited and waited. I have rehearsed a thousand times what I might say should he walk through a door, or appear within a crowd, or materialise one lonely night, sitting on a chair beside a chest of drawers, legs swinging. And now. Now the words desert.

'Yes,' he says. He grins as if he reads my thoughts. 'I've come back. Though, if you remember, I never really went away. Did I Leah?'

He taps my head, then runs his hand down my cheek. I feel the warmth of his blood.

'Adam,' I say. 'I am so glad to see you. I am so glad to see you.'

He smiles once more.

'They say good things come to those who wait,' I say.

'They do not lie,' says Adam.

A silence stretches.

'Tell me a story, Leah. One last time. Tell me a story.'

Now *I* smile, for I know how this will end.

Our eyes lock. I search for words, but I do not pick them out like gems sifted from pebbles, as once I would. This story will be brief. I am ready for the end.

'Once upon a time,' I say, 'there was a girl and a boy. They fell in love. But a shadow darkened them. A shadow of ignorance. Of intolerance. And though they fought it, it was too strong, for they were very young and their power was very small. Even when they were wrenched apart, however, they knew their love would survive. Somehow. Somewhere.'

My voice rises and it fills the room. Adam's touch makes my hand tingle. And as my voice strengthens, the light fades, as if the one is tapping energy from the other.

'They knew they would find a place where they could

be with each other forever. And in that place there would be the people of the past, but now they would be transformed. A woman who understood, finally, that love is in the flesh and in the spirit, that it is infinite and cannot be diminished when others take a part. A man who no longer had to live in nightmares of mud and blood and the death of hope. They would all be together and a dog would rest on their verandah, flick flies away with a lazy tail and dream his dreams. That is the end of my story. And its beginning.'

Somewhere a clock slows. Adam smiles and puts his hand against my cheek once more.

'I have seen that place,' he says.

I grip his other hand tighter.

'Show me?' I say.

Cassie

Holly Holley hates her name, her looks and her life. Then her cousin
Cassie arrives and she has to move out of her bedroom. Life couldn't be
more unfair. But Holly finds a way to stretch her wings. The only question
is, will she fly or will she fall? Book 8 in the Girlfriend Fiction series.

The whole business with Kiffo & the Pitbull

Part quirky journal, part detective fiction, this wild and witty novel is a laugh-out-loud comedy about two unlikely friends who are drawn into a dramatic series of events through their mutual mistrust of the new English teacher.

It's not all about YOU, Calma!

Calma Harrison is in love. But then there's the small matter of the rest of her life, which is fast falling apart. Calma knows the only sure way to shape events is direct, personal intervention. A bold and funny novel about friendship, loyalty and acting on impulse.

Dreamrider

Michael Terny is the fat boy. He's at his seventh school in four years and he knows that he can't change the script. He will be ridiculed and laughed at and pushed around. But Michael has a secret. And then he makes a new friend. Now he can exact his revenge...

Ironbark

Sixteen can be a tough time. And it's almost unmanageable for a wisecracking boy whose temper is white-hot. When he is sentenced to a time-out with his reclusive grandfather in a primitive shack in the Tasmanian forest, the volatile city boy must manage a whole new set of challenges.